MURDER IN A CARE HOME

DAWN BROOKES

Storm

This is a work of fiction. Names, characters, businesses, places, events and incidents are either the products of the author's imagination or used in a fictitious manner. Any resemblance to actual persons, living or dead, or actual events is purely coincidental.

Copyright © Dawn Brookes, 2024, 2025

The moral right of the author has been asserted.

Previously published in 2024 by Oakwood Publishing.

All rights reserved. No part of this book may be reproduced or used in any manner without the prior written permission of the copyright owner. This prohibition includes, but is not limited to, any reproduction or use for the purpose of training artificial intelligence technologies or systems.

To request permissions, contact the publisher at rights@stormpublishing.co

Ebook ISBN: 978-1-80508-943-8
Paperback ISBN: 978-1-80508-944-5

Cover design: Emily Courdelle
Cover images: Shutterstock

Published by Storm Publishing.
For further information, visit:
www.stormpublishing.co

ALSO BY DAWN BROOKES

Lady Marjorie Snellthorpe Mysteries

Murder at the Opera House

Murder in the Highlands

Murder at the Christmas Market

Murder at a Wimbledon Mansion

Murder at the Regatta

Death of a Blogger (prequel novella)

Rachel Prince Mysteries

A Cruise to Murder

Deadly Cruise

Killer Cruise

Dying to Cruise

A Christmas Cruise Murder

Murderous Cruise Habit

Honeymoon Cruise Murder

A Murder Mystery Cruise

Hazardous Cruise

Captain's Dinner Cruise Murder

Corporate Cruise Murder

Treacherous Cruise Flirtation

Toxic Cruise Cocktail

Carlos Jacobi PI

Body in the Woods

The Bradgate Park Murders

The Museum Murders

Memoirs

Hurry up Nurse: Memoirs of nurse training in the 1970s

Hurry up Nurse 2: London calling

Hurry up Nurse 3: More adventures in the life of a student nurse

ONE

The first Monday of the month was one of Lady Marjorie Snellthorpe's favourite days, full of treats. These began with a visit to the hairdressing salon, followed by a manicure, and then she would meet up with a group of friends from the Women's Institute for lunch.

Clara, her hairdresser, smiled when Marjorie entered the salon.

"Good morning, Marjorie."

Marjorie returned the greeting, taking a seat in her usual spot. Clara got to work immediately, setting up the hair rollers for the perm. As she worked, the hairdresser started chatting, filling Marjorie in on the latest gossip.

"Did you hear about Felicity Fothergill? She's been caught shoplifting from that new boutique in town!"

Marjorie raised a sceptical eyebrow, shaking her head. "That sounds hard to believe." But before she could say more, Clara had moved on to another topic of conversation.

"And have you heard what people are saying about you?" A mischievous twinkle appeared in her eyes.

"No. What do they say?"

Clara chuckled softly as she wound another section of Marjorie's hair around a roller and secured it in place. "They're calling you 'The Sleuth of the Manor' – apparently your knack for solving mysteries is becoming well known around here." She winked at Marjorie conspiratorially before returning to her task of rolling up her hair with expert precision.

"I don't live in a manor," Marjorie bantered back.

Thirty minutes later, Marjorie sat beneath a dryer, flipping through a magazine while waiting for her hair to set. This month's gardening supplement was full of photos of happy homeowners tending flower beds. She tried to picture what the gardens would look like in springtime with tulips in bloom and peonies standing proud within cones, and was looking for tips that might inspire her gardener, who loved to experiment.

Last month's reading hadn't been quite so enjoyable, with the only magazine available being one full of celebrity gossip. She had been forced to slog her way through an uninspiring series of stories, ranging from the ridiculous to the more ridiculous. There was a limit to how much interest one could take in the amount of weight a pop singer had gained or how many dates an actor had been seen on.

When she tilted her head under the large dryer and it knocked on one of the curlers, her thoughts strayed from her reading for a little while. The discomfort from the minor bump caused Marjorie to contemplate how so many things had moved on in the past three decades, and yet the cylindrical hairdryer hood remained an immovable stalwart, as sturdy as ever. Although this one was a little less bulky, and far more attractive with its lilac colouring, than the ones she recalled from the late-twentieth century. There might well be more modern contraptions in other hairdressing salons, but she loved this little place in Hampstead and had been coming for... well... decades. It had diversified from being a women's hairdresser to a unisex salon in the year 2000. Her late husband, Ralph, then used to join her and they would often have their hair cut side by side.

Warm memories of his kind face filled her mind. Marjorie's son had always refused to visit the small shop in town because it wasn't glamorous enough for his flashy lifestyle. With her thoughts drifting from new spring daffodils to more weighty matters, Marjorie sighed. It wasn't in her nature to dwell on the negative for long, so she inhaled a purposeful breath, and looked forward to the cup of tea that would follow the removal of her curlers. The time was almost up, according to the clock on the wall opposite.

Marjorie returned her attention to the magazine, and an article about double-flowering hybrid daffodils, but something distracted her from her reading. She sensed a pair of eyes boring into the back of her head. In the mirror's reflection, Marjorie noticed that not just one, but a few heads had turned in her direction. She glanced at the magazine nestled over the handbag on her lap. Gardening magazines weren't usually in high demand, but perhaps she had hogged this one for too long. The woman under the dryer on the opposite side, who had entered with long, wild, frizzy hair, which Marjorie feared had seen too many perms, was making stabbing motions in her mirror. Her face was harsh as her index finger pointed towards Marjorie's lap. Marjorie closed the magazine and held it out to Clara, who was blow-drying another woman's hair in the seat next to her.

"I think the lady behind me would like this," she said, wondering if she was shouting above the noise. She suddenly felt self-conscious, no longer safe in her cocoon, and couldn't hear herself think. All the tranquility and pleasure of her monthly outing had evaporated. Being the centre of attention was not something she enjoyed.

Clara's mouth moved, but Marjorie couldn't hear a word

she was saying with the hot air blowing in her ears, not to mention a drop of water over an eardrum that needed to pop.

The discomfort one has to bear when having one's hair done, she thought.

The woman behind continued her motioning, but whilst Marjorie could see her mouth opening and closing, she couldn't make out her words. Marjorie stared at the magazine again, wondering if there was a valuable coupon inside. She'd read about fights occurring during Black Friday sales and she'd heard of road rage, but was there such a thing as magazine rage? She flipped the pages, but couldn't find a winning lottery ticket or life-changing discount coupon.

Marjorie's eyes pleaded with Clara through the mirror. Clara finished blow-drying and excused herself from the other customer. With a wide grin on her face, she turned to Marjorie and lifted the dryer.

"Your phone's ringing, Marjorie." She swivelled the dryer and turned Marjorie's chair around so that she could hear.

"It can't be, I don't—" She stared down at her handbag and heard the insistent and rather loud ringtone breaking through the comforting noises of the salon.

"Someone's desperate to get you, lovey. They've been ringing for ages."

Marjorie realised that the motioning woman had been pointing to her handbag rather than the magazine. She grimaced.

"At least there's not a crazed new magazine rage." Blasted Jeremy. He'd been to dinner the night before and after giving her the usual lecture about switching her phone on, he must have taken it upon himself to do it for her. She didn't know what annoyed her more, his interference or his rifling through her handbag.

"My son must have turned it on," Marjorie apologised, but the motioning woman had now resumed looking at her own reflection and was chatting to a man next to her. How she could hear above the noise on the other side of the salon was a mystery to Marjorie.

"Why don't I get you a cup of tea while you answer it?" Clara said kindly, turning Marjorie's chair back to face the mirror. "Whoever it is doesn't leave messages."

"I don't switch the answerphone on."

"That would explain it." Clara chuckled. "You get that. I'll finish with this customer and sort you out a nice cup of Earl Grey." Clara took payment from the blow-dried woman at the till, and then headed towards the back room.

Marjorie glared at her handbag, harrumphing. The last thing she wanted to do was to take a telephone call in a public place, especially at the hairdresser's, where gossip spread like a plague. But no matter how long she waited, the persistent ringing continued and was becoming embarrassing as impatient heads turned her way once more.

Why can't people just hang up?

She opened the catch to her handbag and sighed heavily when she saw who was calling. Half-tempted to switch the wretched thing off again, she stopped herself and answered.

"Hello, Edna. I'm sorry, but I'm at—"

"I know you're at the hairdresser's, Marge, your house-keeper told me, but why weren't you answering your phone?"

Marjorie was given no opportunity to answer as Edna's high-pitched trilling continued.

"Never mind about that now. You need to get up here, Marge. Today."

Marjorie removed the phone from her ear, trying to register what Edna Parkinton, her cousin-in-law and friend, was saying, relieved there was nothing wrong with her hearing.

"I don't understand, Edna. We haven't made any arrangements this side of Christmas." Sometimes, Marjorie wondered whether her memory was failing, but she was certain she wasn't due to visit Edna in Harrogate.

"I know that, Marge, but this is urgent. I've checked the trains. There are plenty running today, or you could get Johnson to drive you up here. Something's cropped up. Horace is on his way and I've left a message for your—"

"If you say, 'my Fred' – whose name is Frederick – I'm going to hang up." Marjorie couldn't help noticing a smirk on the face of the next customer being seated beside her.

"Have it your way, Marge, but I'm sure he'll be joining the party when he gets the message. Horace is going to try him again."

Now Marjorie was intrigued. She lowered her voice, softening the tone.

"What's this all about, Edna?"

"Murder, Marge. It's about murder."

TWO

Edna hadn't gone into details over the telephone, not that Marjorie had wanted her to in case half the salon heard. Knowing she was gaining a reputation for sleuthing hadn't been the best news she'd had all year. At least the gossip about her was intriguing, rather than malicious. She hoped this wasn't one of her cousin-in-law's flights of fantasy, but there was nothing to it but to do as Edna asked, or rather, demanded.

It would be nice to see Edna and Horace, and even nicer, if Marjorie was honest, to see Frederick. The autumn months could be such a drag, although she loved the seasonal colour changes. What she didn't enjoy was heating a large house at this time of year. It was challenging knowing which rooms needed to be kept warm.

After taking the call and assuring Edna she would be there later, Marjorie had switched her phone off. Asking Johnson to drive her that distance was out of the question. The poor man had been suffering headaches ever since being coshed at the mansion they had stayed at in Wimbledon a few months before. He argued it was just his eyes needed testing, and he might be right. At least if she went away, he could take some rest and go for an eye test.

Why do men always put health matters off? Ralph was exactly the same. Although, truth be told, she too avoided the doctor like an infectious disease.

After the manic phone call, Marjorie had gone for her monthly manicure and met her friends from the WI for lunch, but Edna's demands had taken all the fun out of both. She was pleased to get home. Before she could concentrate on the sudden change to her schedule, there was a telephone call to make.

Gina Ratton, her housekeeper, brought tea to the drawing room.

"Elsa heard you come in. Oh, your hair looks lovely."

Elsa worked as a housemaid, and she and Gina kept the place clean and tidy. Marjorie didn't need to live in the large house any longer, but she wasn't ready to give it up, nor the memories it held.

"Thank you. I had a call from Edna while I was at the hairdresser's."

"Sorry about that. She rang first thing and said it was urgent. To be honest, I didn't think you'd have your phone on. I was going to tell you she'd phoned when you got back."

Marjorie frowned. "It appears Jeremy took it upon himself to switch the wretched thing on. I'll be the talk of the salon for the next few days."

"You already are," said Gina.

"Oh. You've heard what they're saying, then."

"Don't worry, they only ever say nice things about you, even if you are the Sleuth of the Manor."

Marjorie sighed. "I have to go up to Harrogate for a few days."

"Is Edna all right?"

Marjorie wasn't sure. "I expect so. She's probably decided

she wants company for a while. Horace and Frederick are coming too." At least, she hoped Frederick would come.

"It'll do you good to get away for a bit. The weather's turning and things will be dull around here. We'll keep the place going. Jeremy's got a few dinners booked. Should we go ahead with them?"

Jeremy's habit of using her home for his business entertaining was becoming tiresome, and Marjorie would need to have a word with him at some stage, but not now.

"As long as you don't mind managing it."

"We'll be fine. I'll let Elsa and Johnson know. Give Edna our love, won't you?"

"Of course."

Once Gina left, Marjorie poured tea, picked up the telephone, and dialled. The call was answered after two rings.

"Hello?"

"Felicity, it's Marjorie."

"Hello, Marjorie, how nice to hear from you."

Marjorie wasn't sure how to broach the subject. "I was just thinking about you, so I thought I'd phone and ask how you are."

"To be honest, I've been all of a dither lately. Life's not the same without Bradley."

Felicity Fothergill had lost her husband in the summer to a woman thirty years his junior. Theirs hadn't been a happy marriage, but no-one had seen that one coming.

"I'm sure it must be hard. I'm going away for a few days, but when I come back, why don't we meet for lunch?"

"That would be nice, Marjorie. I've been a bit foolish."

"Really?"

"The police arrested me for shoplifting at that new boutique. I'm surprised you haven't heard. It's all around the village."

Marjorie grimaced. She'd hoped Clara had got it wrong.

"Did you pick something up by mistake? I've been guilty of almost leaving a store with an item in my hands before."

"No. It was quite deliberate." There was a determined tone in Felicity's voice.

"But why? You have everything you need."

"I thought I'd bring shame on that cheating hyena and his piece of trollop. But it backfired."

Marjorie realised she should have been more supportive of her old friend and determined to do better once she got back from Harrogate. Stealing for attention hadn't been on the list of things she thought Felicity capable of, but the woman was clearly suffering.

"I'm sorry to hear that. Will there be charges?"

"No. I returned the next day, apologised, and purchased a whole new autumn wardrobe. They were very understanding and dropped all charges. It was a foolish thing to do and won't happen again."

"That's good to hear," said Marjorie, relieved she could tell Clara the shoplifting episode had been a misunderstanding and put an end to that line of gossip. No doubt there would be some quip about her sleuthing skills, but she could live with that. "I'll call you when I get back from my break."

"I'll look forward to it, Marjorie. Goodbye."

They ended the call and Marjorie looked up to see Johnson, her chauffeur.

"I've booked you an open return train ticket. When you're packed, I'll take you to the station."

"There's really no need."

"You're not carrying suitcases and you're not wasting money on taxis when I'm here."

"Thank you, Johnson. I don't know what I'd do without you."

By four o'clock, Marjorie was on her way to the train station. She had packed a small suitcase, not knowing what to take because she had no idea how long she would be away. Not only did Johnson insist on driving her to the station, but he also wanted to see her safely on the train. She was so fortunate that her employees remained loyal to her, and it was a tribute to how Ralph had treated them.

Marjorie was staring out of the window at the glorious autumnal countryside when she switched her phone back on. She regretted activating voicemail after listening to more rambling but uninformative messages from Edna. The gist was that Marjorie should understand how imperative it was that she *get up here*, as Edna put it. The latest message complained she wasn't already in Harrogate, as at least three trains had been and gone since Edna called, or rather, summoned her. There was a text message from Horace letting Marjorie know he had arrived at Edna's and would keep her calm until Marjorie got there. Another text message was from Frederick, saying he was at a pharmacists' reunion all day, but would arrive at around seven-thirty.

"Perfect," said Marjorie out loud. "We should get there about the same time." She wondered whether to reply to the texts, but wasn't sure she'd manage with all the train's movements. Instead, she sipped tea and read the newspaper.

After putting the paper down, she had an idea. Against her better judgement, she dialled.

"Hello, Marjorie. Have you arrived?" It was good to hear Frederick's voice, even though they spoke most weeks.

"No. I'm on the train from London. I was just wondering where your reunion was?"

"London. Are we on the same train?"

"We must be, as mine arrives at the same time as yours."

"I'll find you. Are you in first class?"

"Erm. Yes." Marjorie knew Frederick wouldn't be travelling first class and felt like a snob.

"See you in a minute."

Marjorie beamed when Frederick appeared through the carriage door. When he saw her, he waved before putting his case in the luggage area.

"If I'd known, we could have travelled together," she said.

"I saw the conductor on the way through the train and upgraded my ticket. To be honest, I thought you were already up there. When I spoke to Edna, she told me you were on your way."

"Edna's interpretation of what I said differs from mine. I had rather a full morning planned, but she wasn't paying much attention. How was your reunion?"

"More of an excuse for drinking, really, but it was good. I caught up with some people I hadn't seen since university days. Pharmacists seem to have a long lifespan."

"I'm pleased to hear it," said Marjorie, noticing Frederick hadn't used the word friends.

"Most of us are long retired, but there are a few who still have their shops. Things are so different now. Back in the day, we used to mix our own lotions and potions. Now they're all bought in."

Marjorie felt that was probably for the best as she couldn't imagine her local pharmacist having the time or the patience to spend mixing substances, and she wasn't sure she would trust them even if they did.

"Funnily enough, I was at the hairdresser's today reflecting on how little has changed for perming hair."

"You'd be surprised," Frederick said. "I remember glyceryl monothioglycolate taking the place of ammonia back in the 1970s."

"I forgot you would be familiar with such things." Frederick was bald himself, but he knew almost everything there was to know about chemicals and pharmaceuticals.

As if reading her mind, he touched his bald head. "I had a perm once in the 1960s. Back when I had hair."

"How intriguing," she said. "Do you have a photo?"

"I expect there's one in an album somewhere. If I find one, I'll send it to you. You'll laugh. Back to the subject of Edna, do you know what's so urgent that we've all been summoned up north?"

"Didn't she tell you?"

"No. The message just said I had to get up to her place, and that you were already on your way. There was another from Horace saying more or less the same thing. What's it all about?"

Marjorie frowned. Edna would well know Frederick had an aversion to murder investigations, and it was dishonest of her not to tell him. Then again, Edna could be overreacting, and there might be nothing to say on the matter.

"I didn't get to hear too much, as I was having my perm when she called."

"And very nice it looks too," said Frederick.

"Thank you." Her hands automatically patted her newly curled locks. "I'm afraid she mentioned the word 'murder'." Marjorie watched the colour drain from Frederick's face. Perhaps she shouldn't have said anything, but she didn't want him to be taken by surprise once they arrived at their destination.

"Murder?"

"That's what she said."

"Who? And what's it got to do with us?"

"I don't have the answer to either of those questions. For all I know, she could be making the whole thing up."

"She wouldn't do that."

"No, she wouldn't. I'm being unfair, but she might be mistaken."

Frederick sighed heavily, looking out of the window. "I guess we'll soon find out."

THREE

After the taxi dropped them off at Edna's house, which was on the outskirts of Harrogate, Marjorie and Frederick gave each other supportive nods. The door opened almost before Marjorie and Frederick had a chance to knock. The lines etched on Horace's forehead spoke volumes about Edna's current state.

"Welcome. It's good to see you both." He popped outside, closing the door behind him, shook Frederick's hand and leaned down to kiss Marjorie on the cheek before lowering his voice. "She's in a bit of a state, so we need to be patient." After opening the door again, he said in a louder voice, "Come on inside. Did you eat on the train?"

"We had a little something." Little was an understatement, Marjorie mused, remembering they had decided not to eat dinner, instead nibbling a few dry biscuits and cheese. She had expected Edna to have dinner prepared, just as she herself would have done had she insisted on guests travelling hundreds of miles.

Frederick placed their suitcases in the hallway before they followed Horace into the cosy but cluttered sitting room. Edna's three-bedroomed house was compact and homely... usually.

There was a musty smell in the room, as if nobody had lived there for some time.

"Has Edna been away?" Marjorie asked.

Horace didn't get the chance to reply as Edna bustled into the room, huffing. "Finally!"

Marjorie would have responded with a sharp retort if she hadn't been so shocked to see, and hear, how breathless her cousin-in-law was. Edna was almost gasping.

"I'm sorry. I had a few prior arrangements to attend to before leaving." Marjorie moved to where Edna had flopped into a wingback lounge chair. She pecked her on the cheek. "I met Frederick on the train."

"So you've told him what this is about, then?"

"I'm not sure I know what this is about, but shall we have some tea, and then perhaps you could explain?"

"Blow the tea, Marge. I've got your favourite brandy in and I know Fred likes a tipple."

"I don't like to drink on an empty stomach," Frederick said, clearly missing the fact there were no cooking aromas.

"Why don't we go to your local pub for dinner?" Horace suggested. "It'll do you good to get out, Edna."

"I'm not hungry," said Edna.

Horace persisted. "You need to eat."

Marjorie had been about to remove her coat, but fastened the buttons again. "What a good idea. Hopefully, it's warm." Edna's house was freezing. Was there a problem with the boiler? Perhaps she was struggling to pay the bills during the cold snap that had fallen upon the nation. It was considerably colder in Harrogate than it had been in London.

Before they left the house, Marjorie noticed Horace going into Edna's kitchen to flip the switch for the central heating. The cold atmosphere couldn't be helping her cousin-in-law's breathing.

Ten minutes later, the four of them were sitting around a

table in a quiet country pub with dinner ordered. Marjorie had been pleased to note that Edna was capable of walking the short distance to her local with no repetition of the chugging breath sounds. Horace got up, insisting he get the drinks in, and arrived back from the bar with a full tray.

Edna perked up. Horace encouraged her, nudging her elbow.

"Get that down you, girl. It'll help."

Marjorie sipped her brandy, not wanting to drink too much before the food came.

They made polite conversation over dinner. Horace held his hand up when Edna tried to say something, making it clear they should eat before they heard whatever story she had to tell. Instead, Edna complained again about how long it had taken Marjorie to catch the train from London, testing Marjorie's tolerance to the limits.

"I told you I had prior arrangements that I couldn't cancel, but I came as soon as I could. Also, I wanted to get a straight-through train and there aren't quite so many of those." Marjorie would have added that dropping everything to take a three-hour train journey was not something she could undertake without a little planning and preparation, but she remembered Horace's warning about patience.

"You've no idea what I've been through, Marge." Edna dropped her knife and fork haphazardly on her plate.

"Please tell us." Marjorie wanted to point out that if she'd finished her meal, Edna should place the cutlery together in the centre of the plate, but she had long since given up on such things. Besides, it would be churlish of her to emphasise etiquette when her cousin-in-law was clearly suffering both physically and emotionally. Was it really just three months since they had been at the Wimbledon tournament?

"Let's get rid of these first. I need another drink."

While the dinner plates were cleared away and Frederick

and Horace went to the bar to buy another round of drinks, Marjorie waited. Once the men returned, she and Frederick looked expectantly at Edna.

"You tell them, Horace."

"Of course." Horace patted Edna on the arm before addressing Marjorie and Frederick. "Edna caught a nasty cold about eight weeks ago, which went onto her chest and turned into pneumonia."

"I ended up in hospital and I can tell you, that's not for the fainthearted these days. The NHS has gone to the dogs." Edna opened her mouth to add more, but didn't have the puff, so closed it again.

Horace took over. "The consultant didn't want her to go straight home, but they needed the bed, so I arranged for her to go into a private care home in the countryside for some rehabilitation."

"I'm sorry, Edna. I didn't know," said Marjorie, feeling guilty.

"No-one did," said Horace. "The hospital insisted on doing some tests and Edna wanted to wait until she had the results in case it was the, erm..." He hesitated.

"You can say the word, Horace. It's not bad luck," Edna said, grinning.

"All right. In case her cancer had returned. The good news is, it hasn't. It was still a nasty case of pneumonia, though. She's recovered now, but the doctor says it might leave her with some scarring on the lungs."

"I'm sorry to hear about all this and I'm pleased you're getting better, Edna," said Frederick. "But Marjorie mentioned something about murder."

Edna cackled. "And they say I speak my mind." Turning more serious, she looked at Horace. "Tell them."

"While Edna was staying at the home, she met a few people who live in the residential accommodation on the grounds. It's a large retirement complex with self-contained apartments and the care home. They use the latter for rehabilitation and for day visitors. I believe they also move people from the flats into the home when they can no longer cope on their own."

Edna interjected. "Horace's right. There are a few long-stay residents in the home, but most are there for rehab like I was. I got to know a few of the people who live in the apartments, those that sing or play instruments and the like. We had singsongs, entertained the poor souls who were stuck in the care home."

Marjorie tried to picture Edna singing in the state she was in. "That's nice. I expect they appreciated that."

Edna couldn't resist a grin. "I've still got it, you know, although I had to use an inhaler before doing any singing."

Marjorie wondered where the inhaler was now, as the breathlessness forced Edna to take another pause. The trio sipped their drinks, waiting for her to recover. Eventually, she looked up.

"Anyway, the reason you're here is that two of my friends have died in the past fortnight. I only found out about the second one this morning when I was leaving. Horace was meeting a friend in Liverpool, so I'd called a taxi to bring me home."

"I can see how that would be upsetting," said Marjorie, "but what's the average age of people living in the home?"

"My friends didn't live in the home. They were self-sufficient in their own apartments. They were knocked off, that's what they were." Edna rubbed her eyes with a handkerchief, causing mascara to smudge.

"We don't know that, Edna." Horace patted her hand, then looked at Marjorie. "They were getting on a bit."

"How old were they?" Marjorie asked.

"Carl was eighty-six and Jackie was ninety-two. But as far

as I know, they were as fit as you and me." Edna snatched her hand away from Horace.

Marjorie didn't think Edna looked that fit at the moment and wondered if their journey had been a waste of time. By the look on Frederick's face, he was thinking the same thing.

"What have the police said?"

"Nothing. They haven't called the police," said Edna. "According to the administrator, the doctor who covers the place signed the death certificates. She said they both died of natural causes."

"And she may be right. What makes you think otherwise?" Marjorie asked.

"I'm telling you, Marge, the two of them were fit and healthy. Carl said he worked out most days, and Jackie could walk for miles. There's a tennis court in the grounds and she still played doubles. What's odd about it is that not long after they made formal complaints, they both snuff it."

Frederick shook his head, eyes scrunched.

Horace took over. "Apparently, there are some factions among the residents. These people lease their properties and pay a lot of additional money for the privileges the complex provides."

"Such as?" Frederick asked.

"Such as very little," said Edna. "They're supposed to have outings, activities, and whatnot, but it's always the same few who get to do what little there is... Them with the most money and the biggest gobs. I didn't really see a lot of them."

Marjorie would have liked to ask whether Edna had established her facts rather than listened to the tittle-tattle, but now wasn't the time. She could ask Horace about that later.

"I've explained to Edna that if you put a load of people our age together in one place, you're bound to get a bit of friction," said Horace. "It doesn't mean anyone's been murdered."

"I'm not saying they were definitely murdered, but it's too

much of a coincidence to me that the two people who got up a petition and were causing the most trouble wind up dead. And not just dead, suddenly dead, if you know what I mean? No illness beforehand, no nothing."

"She has a point," said Horace.

Frederick put his pint glass down on the table before announcing, "Apart from contacting the police and raising your concerns, I can't see what we can do about it."

"That's where you're wrong," said Edna, seeming perky again. "The police won't listen, not when a doctor signed a death certificate, but I've got a plan, and it involves Marge."

Marjorie felt a gnawing in her stomach. Whatever Edna was concocting, it was likely to border on the insane.

FOUR

"That's the most ridiculous idea I've ever heard." Frederick almost choked on his beer when Edna explained what she had in mind. Marjorie also thought it was insane, but was taking more time to mull it over.

Edna snapped back at Frederick, "Well, I can't do it, can I? I've already been in there, and besides that, I asked far too many probing questions before leaving this morning."

"In which case, what makes you think they'll believe you've recommended the home?" Frederick countered.

Edna gave a smug grin. "That one's easy. I can genuinely say I had the best care throughout my stay, and I told the staff that time and time again."

"I still don't like it," said Frederick.

"Then it's a good thing I'm not suggesting you go undercover, isn't it? You'd never be able to keep up the charade... whereas Marge..."

Marjorie was pleased Edna didn't elaborate on why she thought duplicity and lying were competent parts of her repertoire.

"The whole thing is ludicrous." Frederick folded his arms.

"Surely you're not going to agree?" His imploring grey eyes settled on Marjorie's.

"Well?" Edna fixed her with a hard, challenging stare.

"We should all calm down and give Marjorie some time to think about it," said Horace, her suggested co-conspirator. "If you decide to go, Marjorie, I'll be with you every step of the way."

Marjorie couldn't decide whether that was a good or a bad thing.

Frederick's eyes widened as if he was unable to believe that any of them would even contemplate such an audacious plan. "But if you go in too, won't they suspect something's amiss?"

"I've considered that," said Horace. "I intend to tell Craig Tavistock something of what we're doing. He's the owner and I know his father. Craig's not involved in anything shady. I've known him since he was in nappies. If I'm convincing enough, he'll want us to find out whether someone is going around knocking his clientele off."

Edna's jaw dropped. "I don't know that I can agree with that."

"Horace is quite right. It's better if we have someone on the inside who knows what's going on. He might be able to help if we agree to go along with your plan, and if your suspicions turn out to be correct."

"I'm right, Marge, I know I am."

"I'd rather look for evidence and not jump to conclusions."

"You'll do it, then?" Edna stopped arguing.

"On condition you don't interfere, and only do what Horace and I ask you to do. I suggest I go in first and Horace gets admitted the day after. At least that way it will look as though we don't know each other. I assume the staff and residents already know that you and Horace are friends, Edna?"

"Yeah. He visited a lot."

"Good, so it won't look odd if you visit him. Frederick can

be my visitor." She looked at Frederick, who had gone silent. "That's if you're willing?"

A reluctant nod was all he would offer, but it was enough. She knew he would protect her and help where necessary.

"We're on, then?" Horace checked, clearly relishing the idea of another investigation.

"Yes. If Edna believes there's something amiss, the least we can do is look into it." Marjorie only hoped this wasn't one of Edna's flights of fantasy, like her irrational fear of the Loch Ness monster.

"Edna thinks your ability to get people to open up will pay dividends. And when I'm there, we can try to arrange some games evenings or outings."

"At least that would give me the opportunity to check out their flats while they're not in—"

"You'll do no such thing, Edna!" said Marjorie. "If Horace and I are going along with this plan, you must let us decide what needs doing, or we'll all be exposed before we get started."

Edna huffed, but was sensible enough not to push the issue. "Righto, Marge."

Marjorie knew from experience that Edna would not stick to the plan, but if they could keep her meddling to a minimum, they might just stand a chance. She'd leave Horace to manage Edna.

Frederick cleared his throat. "It's all well and good saying you can do all of this, but won't the residents get suspicious?"

"I've thought about that," said Edna, triumphantly. "One of the biggest gripes of the residents is how they don't have enough to do and nothing is organised. They'll jump at the chance."

"We'd be helping them out, and who knows? A place like Evergreen Acres Retirement Homes & Rehabilitation Centre might welcome a few lively inmates with open arms."

"Is that what it's called? My, that is a mouthful," said Marjorie.

Horace chuckled. "It certainly is."

When Marjorie had first met Horace, she'd thought him a show-off who was far too full of himself and had an eye for younger women. The latter might be true, but since they'd become friends, he'd turned out to be just another lonely old man in need of excitement. He had a good heart and was totally dependable when needed, but what made him stand out in her estimation was his ability to handle Edna like no other person in a way that didn't end in confrontation.

Marjorie chucked. "That's settled, then. All we need to do now is decide why I need rehabilitation."

Frederick shook his head. He would hate being put in this kind of situation again, but Marjorie could trust him to do everything possible to help. That's all she could ask of him.

"The awesome foursome are together again," said Edna.

"Sounds like an Enid Blyton novel," said Frederick, forcing a smile.

"Shame we haven't got Hercules with us, then we could be like her famous five." Marjorie grinned as she remembered the friendly Rottweiler who'd stayed for a Christmas break in her home. Imagining him making an appearance in the care home lightened the mood. Marjorie was warming to the idea of going undercover. What better way to while away the autumnal days leading up to Halloween?

"Didn't I mention Apollo?" Edna said.

"I can't believe I'm asking this, but who's Apollo?"

"He's the resident parrot," said Horace. "But be warned. You have to be careful what you say around him. He repeats everything."

"Except he doesn't curse or swear," said Edna, folding her arms.

Frederick looked incredulous.

"She's right," said Horace.

"A Quaker family who couldn't manage him anymore gave

Apollo to the home. They must have taught him what he was and wasn't allowed to say."

Marjorie's eyes widened. "You're serious, aren't you?"

Edna cackled. "It's true. Cross my heart."

"Now I've heard everything. I wonder how they managed to do that."

"Best not to think about it," said Frederick.

"A fall," said Edna.

"The parrot fell?" Marjorie asked, gawping at Edna, wondering if she was losing the thread.

"No, silly. You've had a fall, Marge. You've lost confidence, and that's why you need rehab." Edna smirked when she looked at Marjorie. "Of course, you'll have to get that stick of yours out of your handbag."

Even Frederick laughed at the joke. Marjorie habitually carried a foldaway cane, but hardly ever used it, despite being nagged by her son, her friends, and even her doctor. It came in handy on long walks and when nobody else was around, otherwise it remained tucked away.

"What about Horace?" She deflected the conversation away from herself. "What will be his ailment?"

Horace was fitter than all of them, so it would need to be something convincing.

"How about cataract surgery?" suggested Frederick. "You could simply pretend you had the operation on the day you go in and that you need someone to put your eyedrops in. You can buy a plastic eye patch from a chemist, and I could tape it over one of your eyes. You or one of the staff can take it off the next morning..." He hesitated. "We'd need to get you some pretend drops. Sterile water or saline would do the trick."

"Excellent idea. I see a private guy on Harley Street. He's a Sherlock Holmes buff, goes to mystery nights and all sorts. I'll tell him what we're doing, get him to draft a letter and ask him to courier some eye drops containing water, but labelled as whatever they give you after cataract surgery."

"Just one thing none of you have considered," Frederick added. "What might be a pointless exercise is going to be an expensive charade. I don't expect your manager friend will let you stay for free."

Horace rubbed his chin. "I'll speak to him tomorrow and see if we can sort something out. But don't worry, nobody but me will pay for anything."

"That's kind of you, Horace, but I can't allow you to foot the bill for me. I insist on paying my way. We'll consider it an all-inclusive five-star retreat." Marjorie hated wasting money, but if this turned out to be a situation where they tracked down a killer, it would be worth the expense. She was sure her late husband Ralph would have approved.

"It looks as if you're going ahead with this fiasco, so I'll do what I can to help," said Frederick. "Could someone tell me where I'll be staying?"

"With me," said Edna. "You'll be my guest."

Marjorie had assumed things couldn't have got any worse for poor Frederick, but staying with the combustible Edna would be the meek man's worst nightmare.

"That's settled then." Marjorie offered Frederick as supportive a smile as she could muster. His pallor had returned.

Horace slapped him on the back. "At least I'll be there to protect you for the next two nights."

"Not reassuring," Frederick mumbled, but Horace and Edna had already moved on to discussing the next stage of her master plan.

Marjorie felt a thrill of excitement as she considered her part. She would play it out to perfection, even if it meant using the wretched stick, as Edna called it.

FIVE

Horace had offered to lend Frederick his car to drive Marjorie to the home for her pretend rehab, but Frederick didn't want to take any chances of it being recognised from Horace's visits to Edna.

"People might realise we know each other," he'd argued when booking car hire online. Horace had seen sense and dropped Frederick and Marjorie off to collect the rental car. The hatchback was far less ostentatious than Horace's sports car, although not quite as in keeping with the home they were about to drive into.

As they approached the entrance to the complex, a large sign with gold lettering on a black background made the place look as expensive as it was. Marjorie read out the name Horace had mentioned the night before.

"Evergreen Acres Retirement Homes & Rehabilitation Centre. Why on earth did they choose such a long-winded name?"

"I suppose they need it to sound fancy with the amount of money they are likely to charge."

Frederick had a point. Marjorie had been shocked when

she'd telephoned the home earlier that morning to book her place. The price she was going to be paying was extortionate and, in hindsight, she had wondered whether she should have allowed Horace to pay her fees after all. It wouldn't be unreasonable when he and Edna had been the ones to concoct this plan.

Marjorie could afford the fees, but overnight, she'd had doubts about the soundness of Edna's theory. The two deaths, though sudden, had been deemed natural, and certified as such by a medical professional. The more she thought about it, the less convinced she became that there was some murderous resident or member of staff killing people off.

Perhaps Horace's friend, Craig Tavistock, would give them a discount when he found out about their mission. Alas, Mr Tavistock was away in Dubai at present, so Horace was going to send him an email.

Having driven along the straight driveway, Frederick steered the car around a turning circle, parking in front of a palatial modern building with ample outside seating. To her left, Marjorie eyed the tennis court where the late Jackie had most likely played. To the right of the main building, she saw a sign for a spa.

Marjorie climbed out of the car and noted apartments with front gardens to the left of the care facility. She assumed they were the residential apartments.

Frederick whistled when opening the boot to remove her suitcase. "It's not like any care home I've ever visited. Are you sure about this, Marjorie?"

Marjorie inhaled a deep breath. "It's a little late to back out now."

She glanced around on hearing a leaf blower in the distance, recognising the distinct noise from one her gardener used. The lawns across from the turning circle were immaculately manicured.

A woman stood at the front entrance, holding the door open.

"Let's get you out of the cold," said Frederick, before winking and whispering, "Remember your stick."

Marjorie removed the foldaway walking cane from her handbag and pressed a button, allowing it to spring open. With exaggerated movements, she tottered towards the waiting woman, who was wearing a lilac skirt suit.

"Welcome to Evergreen Acres Retirement Homes & Rehabilitation Centre. I'm Ruby Haigh, the administrator. I hope you had a pleasant journey." Ruby spoke as if by rote, her tone brisk and clipped. No doubt she was responsible for the efficient running of the place, but not the care. If she had to hazard a guess, Marjorie would put the administrator's age as midforties. Black hair, harshly cropped around her face, matched her tone perfectly, although the lilac suit softened her.

"We didn't have far to come," said Frederick. "We stayed in a hotel overnight."

Wishful thinking, thought Marjorie, remembering the sound of Edna's snoring vibrating through the wall all night. Over breakfast, her cousin-in-law had had the audacity to complain that she'd hardly slept a wink, what with worrying whether Marjorie was going to be able to pull off the assigned task. To make things worse, she had suggested it might be better if she developed another bout of pneumonia and did the investigating herself. On the surface, she had sounded convincing when explaining her concern was for Marjorie, but everyone knew she was just worried she might miss out on an adventure, especially as Horace was going to be taking part. Even so, Marjorie had been inclined to let her, but Horace had talked sense into Edna.

"Follow me," said Ruby. "We'll get the paperwork sorted, and then I'll ask one of the staff to give you a tour. You can come back later if you like, Mr—?"

"Mackworth. Frederick Mackworth. I'd rather stay, if that's okay?"

"As you wish." The pasted-on smile slipped a fraction at Frederick not taking her advice.

Marjorie smiled. "I've heard a lot about this place. The online brochure looks magnificent. I'm hoping to be walking a lot more securely by the time I leave."

"We'll have you fighting fit in no time, Lady Snellthorpe—"

"Please call me Marjorie, or Lady Marjorie, if you prefer."

"Lady Marjorie it is, then. How did you hear about us?"

Marjorie had readied herself with an answer that might prompt an early reaction. "It was through a friend of a friend. My friend told me her friend has accommodation here. I must give her Beryl's regards when I meet her."

"Oh? Which one of our residents does your friend know?"

Marjorie forced her brow to furrow, as if trying to remember. "Oh dear... the memory isn't what it was... Erm... Oh, yes! Jackie something or other – I don't always recall surnames."

The reaction was courteous and professional, giving nothing away. "I'm so sorry, your friend obviously hasn't heard. Miss Bagshaw passed away yesterday."

"Oh dear, I'm sorry to hear that. Beryl said she spoke to her on the telephone a week ago and she was well. Was it sudden?"

"It was, but I always say at that age I'd rather go suddenly, wouldn't you?"

"Indeed. How old was she?"

"Ninety-two."

Not too many years from my age, thought Marjorie, who never considered herself an old woman.

"Would you like me to let your friend know?" Ruby asked.

"Oh no, dear. I'll tell her when I next speak to her. They only spoke now and then. Funny how it was just recently they last communicated, but at least she can remember whatever it was they spoke about. I'll let you know if she wants the funeral details, but she lives on the south coast. It's a long way to travel."

"Yes. Right. Now, shall we get on?" Ruby seemed keen to end the conversation and had been matter of fact about the death of one of her long-term residents. Perhaps with the independent living arrangements, she didn't get so involved. One couldn't expect staff to burst into tears each time an elderly person died, although Marjorie couldn't imagine the stiff and starchy Ruby Haigh bursting into tears over anything. A gentle dab of the eye would be more her style, assuming she ever cried.

Marjorie was still thinking about this when Ruby came to an abrupt halt. A man in a wheelchair was speeding towards them. She bristled, turning to Marjorie.

"That's Mr Butler. I'm sure you'll be introduced later, but we should avoid him for now. And whatever you do, don't ask him how he is."

Too late. He was already upon them. "Good morning, Darren. I just need to go through some paperwork with this lady. Can it wait?"

"I don't think so. I've got terrible pains in my abdomen. The last time I had pain like this, the doctor said it was the worst case he'd ever come across."

"Worst case of what?" Frederick asked, drawing a glare from Ruby.

"I can't remember. It was such a long name... Very rare, you know. I'm one of life's mysteries. That's what the surgeon said when he opened me up. Nearly died on the table, I did. Every illness I get is worse than any other case the doctor's ever seen..."

Darren Butler droned on, seemingly proud of all his ailments and mishaps, which he described in great detail, although most of them lacked a firm diagnosis. When they heard a tea trolley approaching, Ruby took her opportunity.

"Tea's here, Darren. Come with me, Lady Marjorie."

"Lady, eh?" Darren tipped a pretend cap. "Pleased to meet you. I hope you're staying. We haven't had any aristocracy lately, not since—"

Marjorie didn't get to hear who the last aristocrat had been, because a uniformed man appeared. "Let's get you some tea, Darren," he said, whisking the wheelchair away. "You know how the doctor says it's good for you."

"Mr Butler lives in an apartment, but he spends more time in here than at home. He's not half as ill as he thinks he is, but we try to be good listeners."

I hadn't noticed, thought Marjorie.

"Does his wife live here?" Frederick asked.

"She used to, but she died five years ago. I would avoid the subject if I were you. I don't mean to sound unkind, but he can talk about his grief for even longer than his infirmities."

"It sounds as though he's had a lot of hospital stays," said Marjorie.

"He hasn't seen a doctor, other than for our regular health checks, in three years."

"A hypochondriac, then." Marjorie turned to whisper to Frederick. "But more importantly, a talker. I think I need to get to know Darren Butler."

With the paperwork signed and a telephone call to her bank to transfer a painful amount of money into the organisation's coffers, Marjorie was dismissed to a waiting area with Frederick.

"If you would stay here, someone will be along shortly."

Ruby left them sitting in comfortable armchairs where they were provided with tea and biscuits.

"What do you make of it so far?" Marjorie asked Frederick once Ruby was back in her office.

"Expensive," said Frederick. "I hope Edna appreciates what you're doing for her. And I hate to say it, Marjorie, but I'm also convinced that you're wasting your money."

MURDER IN A CARE HOME 33

Frederick was pessimistic by nature, but Marjorie understood where he was coming from. Hopefully, she could be in and out in a few days, although she'd had to commit to a four-night stay, the minimum term allowed.

"I hope you're right and it turns out to be nothing, but now I'm here, I'm going to find out what happened to Edna's friends."

"Ruby Haigh didn't seem to care much, did she?" Frederick remarked. "I wonder how long Jackie had lived here. And what happens to their apartments after they die?"

"Both good questions and ones I'd like to get an answer to. All we know about Jackie and the man, Carl, from what Edna told us, is that they were stirring up trouble. Perhaps you could ask her for more details when you get back. And also ask her who, if there was anyone else, they were close to. She said there was a group that played instruments or sang, which implies there were more than two. It was too late to ask last night, and I was too tired this morning. I didn't sleep that well."

"You heard the bear as well, then?"

"Don't tell me you could hear her from downstairs?"

"Indeed, I could."

They both jumped when a shrill voice squawked, "EDNA! HEAR HER DOWNSTAIRS! EDNA!"

"My goodness!" Marjorie's hand flew to her chest. "That must be Apollo."

"No wonder he's called Apollo. He's got a cry that commands attention."

In a large cage was the most beautiful parrot Marjorie had ever set eyes upon. If he'd been a human, he would have been a model.

"APOLLO! APOLLO!" the bird screeched again.

Marjorie lowered her voice. "Remember, we have to be careful what we say or he'll give us away."

"Give us away, he will. Give us away." This time, the bird's message was lower as he decided to chomp through some food at the same time.

Frederick took Marjorie's arm and led her to the other side of the waiting area. Anxiously looking towards Apollo, he whispered, "And now we know he's got perfect hearing."

Marjorie whispered back, "Any other time, I might be happy to meet Apollo, but now we know where his cage is, we'll tread more carefully."

She glanced over at the parrot, who appeared to be sizing her up with an I-know-what-you're-up-to look. A nervous chuckle rose in her throat as she shook the thought from her head.

SIX

Just when Marjorie was tiring of sitting, a pot-bellied man with sandy brown hair, thinning on top, hurried towards them.

"I'm sorry to have kept you waiting. I'm Peter Grabham, the senior nurse. We try not to be too formal here. Most people call me Pete."

Marjorie took the outstretched hand and noted his handshake was firm and confident. Pete wore a crisp white tunic over dark brown trousers. The tunic was a little too tight over the belly. Whether his paunch was because of beer or food, she wouldn't surmise. What remained of his hair was neatly combed back.

Pete's manner was easy and warm with an engaging smile which, unlike Ruby's, reached his dark brown eyes. That said, worry lines hung around, even with the friendly greeting.

"How do you do? I'm Marjorie Snellthorpe. This is my friend Frederick Mackworth."

"Pleased to meet you both. Welcome to our home, Lady Snellthorpe," he said, the sound of his voice a steady baritone.

"I'm not one for formality either. Please call me Marjorie."

"Of course. I believe you'll like the facilities here, Marjorie, so allow me to show you around." Pete ushered them from the waiting area into a large lounge – a sitting room where a group of people, including Darren Butler, were still drinking tea. Some were reading newspapers, others magazines or books. A black and white cat was nestled on a petite woman's knee while she read.

"It's nice that you allow pets."

Pete's eyes followed Marjorie's gaze. "That's Timmy. He came from a local cat rescue after the manager read an article on pet therapy. He's popular with all the outside residents and some of our rehab clientele, but the former overfeed him."

"He looks in perfect shape to me," said Frederick.

"Cook intends to keep it that way since she's taken on responsibility for his authorised feeding after the resident who used to do it passed away. She plans to give him a weekly weigh-in and adjust his diet accordingly."

"My, my," said Frederick, grinning. "We should all follow her lead. I'm fond of cats myself and I know what you mean about pet therapy. I read that stroking pets lowers the blood pressure."

"So they say," Pete muttered. Marjorie got the impression Pete wasn't as fond of felines as the residents were.

The tour continued, with Marjorie and Frederick following Pete Grabham through a maze of corridors and communal rooms. Each room they entered was fully equipped with modern amenities, from the latest exercise apparatus to relaxing lounge chairs, most of which reclined. Pete showed them inside a well-stocked modern library with a vast selection of books and a gorgeous domed skylight.

As he waxed lyrical about every room, it became obvious how proud he was of Evergreen Acres and its facilities. Marjorie and Frederick continued following him as he showed them first one dining room, then another.

"Most of our rehab clients use the larger dining room and

the few of our external residents who come in for meals eat in the smaller one. There's no rule on where you eat. You can pick. We even offer room service if you ever need your own space."

"It's all very impressive," said Marjorie.

"Visitors can stay for meals for a small charge." Pete looked at Frederick.

"That might be useful," Frederick replied.

"If you have any special dietary requirements, you can tell Cook. You'll soon discover how varied the menus are and how sumptuous the food is. I even eat here myself when I'm on duty, which is most of the time, if I'm honest."

That answered the question of the paunch, Marjorie noted to herself. She watched their host pat his rounded middle and checked for a wedding ring. There wasn't one.

"I eat most things, so I don't think there will be any problems as far as food is concerned," she replied.

"Who's that austere looking man who keeps marching around?" Frederick asked.

Marjorie and Pete turned to see who Frederick was referring to. A skinny man, just a little taller than Frederick, with shoulder-length shaggy grey hair, wearing ill-fitting clothes and a frown on his face, was moving backwards and forwards. Marjorie would have described his pacing as shuffling rather than marching, but she could see what Frederick meant.

"That's Victor, Victor Redman. He's one of our apartment residents and a former detective inspector. Don't mind him. He likes to think he's still on duty."

Marjorie studied the man called Victor before turning back to Pete. "It must be reassuring to have someone like him around. I expect it would make the others feel safe and secure."

"I don't know about that. Victor's eighty-five and has Parkinson's disease, but he believes he's responsible for the residents' security. Not that it's needed, you're quite safe here." Pete winked. "Still, Victor takes his protection duty seriously, and it gives him something to occupy himself. Now, let me show you the gym, as you'll be spending a fair amount of time in there."

Marjorie's heart sank, and her eyes widened. "Will I? I'm sure that won't be necessary."

"All our fall clients spend time in the gym, Marjorie. Hannah is most insistent they do."

"Hannah?"

"Our resident physiotherapist. You'll meet her this afternoon. She'll be keen to get you to work as soon as possible."

Marjorie felt her stomach churn. "Today?"

"We aim to give you the treatment you're paying for, Marjorie." Pete's tone had changed from amicable to condescending within seconds, and Marjorie felt a power shift.

Frederick's eyes crinkled as he nudged her. "Perhaps when you've spent some time with Hannah, you won't need your cane." He really had a wonderful face when he laughed, although Marjorie was struggling to see the funny side of spending her time in a gymnasium. Her young friend Rachel, a fitness fan, would find it hilarious when she told her.

"Oh, it would be splendid to get rid of this thing," she murmured, waving the cane around, but her voice sounded unconvincing.

"Hannah's excellent at what she does," said Pete. "You never know, Marjorie. Miracles do happen."

Marjorie felt her lips tighten. She was regretting giving him permission to use her name without the title. She'd foolishly imagined it would be easy to impersonate a frail elderly woman in need of a confidence boost, but at that moment, she wanted to yell at him or give him a whack with her cane. The desire to tell him she was in perfectly good health and didn't need to be spoken to like a child was almost overwhelming.

"Hmm," was the only word she could force out of her mouth.

Frederick nudged her again, putting his finger to his lips, as if able to read her mind.

"Don't."

After spending far too long pretending to admire the gymnasium and its treadmills, bars, weights and a piece of equipment Pete told her was a cross trainer, which looked more like a torture machine, Marjorie had had enough.

"Why can't people just go for a walk?" she whispered to Frederick.

"Are there many good walks around here?" Frederick asked Pete.

"Yes, there are. Let me show you outside. We can pick your coats up on the way."

Marjorie and Frederick had hung their coats in the visitors' area while they were waiting for the tour to start after finding the heat inside stifling. They collected them, Marjorie ignoring a cackle from Apollo. She was certain that bird could read minds.

Pete escorted them outside, where she felt more at home. The grounds were immense and the gardens well-tended, although the large leaf-covered pond was murky. It was good to see some of the clientele enjoying the fresh air. A few people nodded greetings.

"It's gorgeous out here. I hope Hannah feels walks in the fresh air are also therapeutic," Marjorie said.

Pete stifled a laugh, shaking his head. "I'll be sure to mention it to her," he said, not sounding at all convincing.

Marjorie had a feeling she and Hannah would not be on the same page when it came to her exercise regime. Hopefully, she could get her investigating underway, and then experience the miraculous recovery Pete had joked about.

The senior nurse didn't appear to be fond of the fresh air himself, and after an all too brief meander, they were led back inside.

"I forgot to mention that as well as Hannah, the home employs personal trainers, dieticians, and massage therapists. We have a hairdresser who comes in once a week and a podiatrist who visits every fortnight. You might not meet him as he's already been this week."

No doubt these people attract a surcharge, thought Marjorie. "Such luxury. I'll be spoilt for choice."

"We like to think we've got everything, but if you find there's something missing, don't hesitate to mention it and we'll see what we can do. Our local GP also does a round once a week."

"What about activities and outings?" Frederick asked. It impressed Marjorie how well Frederick was embracing the subterfuge.

"It's funny you should mention that. We've struggled of late to get regular activity coordinators, but we're working on it."

Marjorie gave Horace and his idea of organising an outing an internal thumbs up.

"The owners and our administrator, Ruby, are looking around for someone."

"An outing would be so therapeutic," said Marjorie. "I've missed getting out since the fall."

Pete nodded sympathetically. "It will also solve one of our problems and major bugbears from the permanent residents if we can find the right company," he said. "We almost had a mutiny on our hands over the summer."

"Really?" Marjorie said.

"I'm exaggerating, but we had a few people who were unhappy."

"Had?" Marjorie jumped at the opportunity to probe.

"Sadly, two of the ringleaders have recently passed away. To be honest, most of us miss their feistiness."

"But not all?" Frederick asked.

Pete seemed to realise he had said more than he meant to.

"We all miss them. Anyway, we take our commitments to our residents and clients seriously, so it will be good to resolve that one issue soon. You'll find everything else is in order."

Frederick and Marjorie nodded in unison. Marjorie was deep in thought. Could there be more substance to Edna's suspicions than she'd given her credit for, or was it a case of people aiming to get what they were paying for?

They had barely finished the tour when a gong sounded. "That's lunch, we're a bit later than usual today," said Pete. "Would you like to stay, Frederick? The first meal's on the house."

"I'd love to. Thank you."

"I'll have your suitcase taken to your room, Marjorie, and make sure someone shows you which room's yours after you've eaten." Pete spread his hands to encompass the extensive building. "I'll leave you to choose a dining room."

The senior nurse scuttled away, leaving them standing on the edge of the expansive sitting room. Marjorie was on the move almost immediately. She had a target in her sights and marched towards him.

Frederick caught up with her, placing a hand on her elbow. "Slow down, Marjorie. Remember, you're supposed to have mobility problems."

"Whoops, so I have." She grinned, but did as instructed and brought her cane down from where it had been waving in the air like a conductor's baton to the floor. "I didn't appreciate being spoken to as though I've lost my marbles."

"You should have seen your face when he mentioned gym work. I was worried you were going to put him in his place."

Marjorie chuckled. "Don't you worry, I'm looking forward to having that pleasure once our work here is done."

"Where are you heading to in such a hurry, anyway?"

"I want to see if we can have a word with that ex-detective inspector. Victor Redman, wasn't it?"

SEVEN

"Do you mind if we join you?"

Marjorie had been determined to speak to Victor Redman since Pete had mentioned his former occupation. He was a dour-looking man with a thin face and his baggy suit hung off him. That and his hollowed-out cheeks suggested he had suffered recent weight loss.

Sitting at a round table set for four people, with a floral tablecloth and a bud vase containing fresh irises, Victor was gazing out of the window at a shrubbery when Marjorie interrupted him. A bustling bird-feeding station, strategically placed for maximum visibility, added a touch of liveliness to the otherwise quiet surroundings outside. Blue tits and goldfinches were helping themselves to the sunflower and niger seeds.

Victor's green eyes narrowed. "Free country. Do what you like." He then glared around the room as if sizing up each individual daring to enter and finding them lacking.

Up close, he appeared even more frail and gaunt than he had done from a distance. It reminded Marjorie of an old friend who had suffered from Parkinson's disease. Their once vibrant body had slowly wasted away until they were nothing but skin and bones. Thankfully, the treatments had moved on since then, although there was still no cure.

Frederick offered his hand. "I'm Frederick. This is Marjorie, she's going to be staying for a few days."

Victor shook the hand and motioned for them to sit. "Victor Redman. Don't worry about your friend, I'll keep an eye out for her." Although his voice was gruff, it had a tenderness to it.

Marjorie held back her displeasure at being spoken about as if she weren't there, taking a seat and instead saying, "That's comforting to know. I've never stayed in a care home before."

"This ain't your typical care home, that it ain't," said Victor. "But don't you worry, I'll make sure nothing happens to you."

"That's good of you, but I'm sure nothing's going to happen to me," said Marjorie.

"Sure, are you? Well, I wouldn't be quite so confident if I were you." Victor's eyes were fixed somewhere in the distance, not looking at her even though he was addressing her.

Frederick stepped in before she could ask what he meant by his last remark. "Do I detect an Irish accent? I have distant relatives in Cork."

"I'm originally from Dublin, but I've lived this side of the Irish Sea for fifty years now. Me mam used to say you never lose the accent yer born with. She was right about most things, was me mam. What about you? Where do you hail from?"

"I live in Bath, but spend a lot of my time in the north these days. Marjorie here lives in London."

"Judging by the accent, she comes from the posh part as well."

Marjorie had had quite enough of being talked about and answered before Frederick took it upon himself to speak for her.

"I live on the edge of Hampstead Heath, as a matter of fact."

"Why didn't you go to a posh home down there? I assume you're here for rehab."

Marjorie could tell that Victor Redman remained astute and

had all his faculties, despite Pete implying he might not have. "I was on holiday up here when I had a fall. Frederick was kind enough to search the internet and found this place. It has excellent reviews."

"That's as may be, but you need to watch out. Things ain't what they seem."

At that moment, an elegant woman, who was immaculately turned out, took the vacant seat at their table. She wore carefully applied makeup and had silver-grey hair hanging in waves down to her shoulders. She smiled at Marjorie and Frederick before chastising their table companion.

"Now, Victor, don't start going on about your conspiracy theories again! Especially not with newcomers. They might believe you."

"This is Isabelle Stoppard," said Victor. "Marjorie here's in for rehab after a fall, and this is her friend, Frederick."

Excellent memory, Marjorie computed. "How do you do?" she said to Isabelle.

"I'm well, thank you. I hope Victor's not frightening you. He's an ex-detective inspector and still sees criminals behind every tree." She shot Victor a disapproving but affectionate look.

"How interesting," said Marjorie, "to meet a former detective. I bet you have some stories to tell."

"I do, but they're wasted around here. Nobody listens. They wouldn't know a criminal until they were choking the last breath out of them."

"That's enough of that kind of talk, Victor. Take no notice of him. He resents not being able to lord it over people anymore, that's all. He was a stickler for discipline back in his day."

"At least I didn't spend my working life tittle-tattling. Couldn't you find anywhere else to sit?"

"As a matter of fact, I had plenty of more friendly offers. Why I choose to sit with you every day is a wonder even I can't fathom."

Marjorie couldn't work out whether this was the kind of banter she and Edna shared, or whether there was a little animosity between the two. No doubt all would be revealed. She was still mulling it over when a woman who appeared to be in her forties, wearing a deep purple uniform and a large purple hat, arrived at the table.

Looking at Marjorie, she beamed. "Welcome to Evergreen Acres. I'm Patsy Prindle, but everyone calls me Cook. I like to meet all our newcomers, and I gather you're staying with us for a few days?"

"Thank you, I am. I'm Marjorie and this is my friend, Frederick. I'm booked in for four days at present."

"You'll like it here; the facilities are amazing. Do you have any special dietary requirements?" The buxom woman had an open stance and beautiful smile with the whitest teeth Marjorie had ever seen.

"I eat most things. Frederick has to watch his blood pressure, so nothing too salty for him." Marjorie shot Frederick a triumphant look. It was her turn to speak for him.

Cook, however, gave him a sympathetic look. She handed them both menus that wouldn't have been out of place in a five-star restaurant.

"Have a browse through these. I'll be back in five to take your orders."

Marjorie's eyes scanned the menu before turning to Isabelle. "Any recommendations?"

"Everything Cook prepares is delicious, which is one reason I eat here—"

"That and the fact she's never cooked a meal in her life," Victor interjected.

"There is that." Isabelle grinned before returning to the subject. "I highly recommend the lamb tagine. It's like nothing you've ever tasted before."

"Lamb tagine it is, then," declared Marjorie. She turned to Frederick. "What about you?"

Frederick's eyes were widening as he perused the menu. It couldn't be that the options overwhelmed him. They had eaten out a lot; it must be the situation.

"Um... I'm not very hungry. I'll just have soup."

Isabelle clucked disapprovingly. "You don't know what you're missing."

As Cook returned to take their respective orders, aromas of rich flavours wafted through the dining room, preparing the taste buds for what was to come. Cook added her own disapproving look into the mix when Frederick reiterated he only wanted soup.

The residents at other tables were enjoying three-course cuisine, but when Victor's dinner arrived, it was a soft mushy stew. The dish was garnished to look as good as it could, but it was not comparable to the attractive lamb tagine arriving a few moments later.

Victor's brows furrowed as he stared down at the unappetising meal in front of him. "How's a grown man supposed to survive on this?" he grumbled, his voice laced with frustration.

"It has all the nutrients, Victor. You know they have only softened it for easier consumption. Do you need me to help you?" Isabelle clearly cared for the stubborn ex-detective.

"I can manage on my own, thank you," he retorted, but there was a hint of gratitude in his tone. "Isabelle's ninety but likes to think she's a thirty-year-old," he added with a throaty snigger.

Marjorie recognised the two of them had a unique dynamic. She couldn't believe the woman, who didn't look a day over seventy, was ninety. Marjorie prided herself on looking a lot younger than her eighty-something years, but Isabelle was something else.

"What was it you did for a living?" Frederick asked Isabelle, deflecting the conversation away from Victor while he struggled to eat his food. It was obvious he had trouble swallowing, but was too proud to say anything. Other than that, and the weight loss, he had few symptoms of the degenerative disease he was suffering.

"I was a journalist. Not a tittle-tattle journalist, although Victor likes to tease me. I worked for *Vogue* magazine."

"Celebrities R Us," Victor mumbled, forcing a grin. His teeth, unlike Cook's, were yellow and brown. Marjorie surmised they were stained from many years of tobacco use.

"That joke's as old as you are, Victor Redman," Isabelle scolded.

"He liked it," Victor said, defensively, motioning towards Frederick who was still grinning.

"You must have met many interesting people in your time," said Marjorie. "I hope we get to hear about some of them."

"Yeah, come on, Isabelle, let's have a bit of name-dropping."

Isabelle finished the last mouthful of lamb before replying with a faraway look in her eyes. "Too many to remember them all, but I'm sure you would recognise the names of some people I interviewed. I once had to do a piece on Elizabeth Taylor. A most interesting woman. Not at all like I'd imagined."

Isabelle entertained them with stories of minor and major celebrities and models, along with some of the quirkier moments she'd dealt with, such as an actress who insisted on being interviewed alongside a teeth-baring Doberman.

"That was one of the quickest interviews I ever did, the saving grace being that it wasn't for television, otherwise it would have been punctuated with snarls. Almost like having lunch with Victor."

Marjorie laughed with her, and even Victor smiled. What Marjorie liked most about Isabelle was that whilst she could have done, she didn't brag.

"How did you get into journalism in the first place?" Frederick asked.

Isabelle looked away, covering her face with a hand.

"Headache again?" enquired Victor.

"I think so. I've probably done too much this morning."

"I sympathise," said Marjorie. "I'm a migraine sufferer."

Victor patted Isabelle's hands. "These blasted things come on her so suddenly and much more frequently these days, and the heat in here doesn't help. You should rest, Isabelle."

Their conversation had clearly concluded, but it would have been ended anyway when a member of staff came to the table to tell Marjorie it was time to show her to her room. She also told her she had an appointment with Hannah, the physiotherapist, for an assessment at three o'clock. Marjorie frowned on hearing the appointment was in the gymnasium.

Isabelle grinned. "Oh dear. I wish you luck with that one."

"You'll need it," added Victor. "Hannah would be a challenge for Isabelle's Doberman."

Marjorie wanted to ask what they really thought of the physiotherapist, but the young woman waiting for her seemed eager to get on.

"I'll head off to the, erm... hotel," said Frederick. "I'll be back to see you tonight."

Marjorie was sorry to watch Frederick go, suddenly feeling alone and vulnerable. It left her playing a part she hoped she could fulfil.

As she followed her escort, who was around twenty-five and introduced herself as a care assistant called Diana Ferrett, Marjorie reflected on the conversation she and Frederick had enjoyed over lunch. It was easy to see why Isabelle and Victor, who were complete opposites, got on so well. They both had excellent memories, sharp focus, and enquiring minds. Surely, they would have noticed if something was off about the two former residents' deaths? Victor had implied that something was amiss, but Isabelle had suggested he was purely hankering after his old life. Was she right or was there something in what he said?

Straightening her shoulders, along with her determination, Marjorie intended to find out if there was anything to Edna's suspicions or if she was overreacting.

EIGHT

The door to the gymnasium was ajar. Marjorie peered through the gap, a slight tremor coursing through her body like it was her first day at school. The memory of that day flooded her mind with vivid clarity.

A tall and imposing woman stood silently, staring at something through a large window, her features stern. Marjorie's fingers traced the embossed letters on the card she had found in her room, confirming the appointment the carer Diana had mentioned. The woman hadn't noticed Marjorie, so she rapped her knuckles against the door.

The woman didn't move, but with an authoritative voice, she called, "Enter."

Marjorie inhaled deeply before pushing the door open. She put one foot inside, bracing herself for whatever lay ahead.

When the woman turned, Marjorie noticed the crisp white tunic was adorned with a name badge bearing golden lettering on a jet-black background – the same branding as the sign that greeted visitors at the entrance of the facility. It told Marjorie this was the physiotherapist she was here to meet.

Hannah McManus was statuesque, rigid almost, with long,

artificially coloured brunette hair cascading halfway down her back. As Marjorie crossed the threshold, she squinted, trying to catch a glimpse of the eyes hidden behind thick layers of black mascara and dark brown eyeshadow. What caught her attention was the physiotherapist's bright red lips, perfectly shaped into a fullness that gave the impression they had been enhanced by some form of cosmetic surgery. Hannah's lips stood out from her otherwise narrow face, adding the only glamour to her appearance.

When Marjorie got closer, Hannah peered down at her, revealing an upturned nose and a posture exuding superiority. Marjorie felt tiny, her small figure hunched, shrinking under Hannah's gaze. Sometimes her five-foot-nothing frame made her feel inferior, and this was one of those occasions.

"Take a seat."

Marjorie couldn't tell whether there was an attempted smile from the immobile mouth. She cautiously took a seat on a plush, muted-green chair, checking for a hint of warmth in the eyes, but saw there was none.

"Pleased to meet you," Marjorie tried, but got no response.

Hannah sat down herself, her attention fixed on a manila folder spread open across her desk. Marjorie averted her eyes from the imposing exercise equipment and waited expectantly.

"Mm, Lady Marjorie Snellthorpe," Hannah murmured, flipping through pages. "I see you've had a recent fall." Not waiting for a reply, Hannah continued reading. "Lost confidence and in need of rehab. Mm..."

The dyed brunette eyebrows, matching her hair, furrowed. Perhaps only the mouth had been treated so far.

Hannah's lips tried to move into a pout as she once more peered down at Marjorie from what seemed like an unnecessarily lofty chair. The physiotherapist not only had a height advantage, but the added benefit of an adjustable seat. If it was meant to make Marjorie feel even smaller, it was working. The chair creaked slightly as Hannah shifted her weight, causing Marjorie to wonder just how much higher it could go.

"That's correct." Marjorie's usually confident voice lacked its authority and rang tremulously in her own ears. She shifted in the stiff, uncomfortable chair as the no-nonsense Hannah finally appeared to concentrate on what she was doing and put more than a few words together.

"Don't worry, Lady Snellthorpe, I'll have you back on your feet in no time."

Marjorie resisted the temptation to confess that this was all an act and she was already on her feet, if not precisely at that moment. A small grin tugged at the corners of her mouth before fading just as quickly when she noticed Hannah's scowl.

The physiotherapist abruptly pushed her chair back and stood up. "Let's get on with it, shall we?"

"Now?" Marjorie questioned, dreading what might come next.

A sharp tut escaped Hannah's lips, followed by another furrowed brow and "Mm". Marjorie could tell this was the only answer she was going to get. With a deep breath, she mirrored Hannah's movements, apart from the chair pushing, and stood.

"I'm not sure I'm up to anything too strenuous at the moment."

Hannah simply waved away her protest with a casual flick of the wrist, closing in on Marjorie with determination.

"Arms up above your head," she commanded.

Marjorie would have liked to refuse, but instead obliged, feeling a creak in her right shoulder and a stretch in her muscles as she did so. There followed an intense twenty minutes filled with clipped orders:

"Hands on hips…"

"Twist…"

"Lean forward…"

"Now back…"

Hannah's swift movements barely gave time for a response before she moved on to the next.

"Touch your toes..."

Marjorie didn't budge.

"Well?"

"I haven't touched my toes since I was at school, so I don't think I'm going to do that now."

"Mm." Hannah stopped there, concluding her assessment. Her clinical approach had been clear throughout. Pausing to explain or involve Marjorie in the process was not her style. Instead, she had snapped her orders, written notes in the folder, and returned it to the desk with a final satisfied "Mm", which seemed to be Hannah's favourite word.

Marjorie remained standing, not sure whether to sit down again. Hannah broke the silence.

"I see what the problem is. You have muscle wasting in your legs and upper arms. But don't worry, we'll address that soon enough."

Marjorie bit her tongue, trying her hardest not to argue. She couldn't imagine Edna conforming to Hannah's authoritative style and was keen to ask her cousin-in-law how the two of them had got on.

"I see." She forced the reply.

"And you've most likely lost height." She gave Marjorie a pitying look, as if she couldn't imagine anyone being so short for their entire life. Alas, in Marjorie's case, she had never experienced the growth spurts most people did. Other than when faced with top shelves in the supermarket, her height was rarely a disadvantage, but in the face of Hannah's condescending tone, it was under threat.

She threw her shoulders back and fought her corner. "I've only lost half an inch. Doesn't everyone lose a little height as they grow older?"

"Mm. You need a programme of physical exercise. I'll write

a plan and one of my assistants will show you what to do. You'll also need a DEXA scan."

"What's that?" Marjorie knew what it was, but wanted to see if Hannah's vocabulary extended beyond just a few words.

"Dual Energy X-ray Absorptiometry." Noting Marjorie's blank look, she added, "It measures your bone density. We can do it here... There will be an additional charge..."

Of course there will, thought Marjorie. "Is the scan necessary?"

"Mm... Everyone of your age should have one. I'm surprised you haven't had multiple scans by now..."

Marjorie sighed. *I'll be having a chat with my GP when I get home.*

"You've most likely got balance problems due to osteoporosis, that's why you're falling."

Marjorie wanted to point out that she had only suffered one *fictional* fall and, other than that, she was in perfect health. She walked every day, took a daily dose of vitamin D in the winter months and was no more likely to have osteoporosis than the officious physiotherapist in front of her.

What she said was, "I suppose it's best to check."

"Mm... I'll arrange for you to have the scan in the morning. Your exercise regime can start after that. In a day or two, you can join the group classes we hold daily. I'll also arrange a blood workout. There'll be an extra—"

"Cost," Marjorie finished. She was even more determined to find out what Edna thought of Hannah McManus and was slightly annoyed her cousin-in-law hadn't warned her.

"Mm... Right... We're done for today." The folder snapped shut.

"You haven't asked me about the fall," said Marjorie. The card had said her appointment was for forty-five minutes and she was determined to eke the last ten out of her oppressor.

Hannah raised an eyebrow, sighing as she opened the folder

again. With pen aloft, and not speaking, she waved a go-on-then hand at Marjorie.

Now she was on the spot, Marjorie didn't know what to say. She hadn't thought it through and hated lying even more than wasting money.

"Actually, I'd rather not talk about it. It's too upsetting."

The folder slammed shut again.

"Is there anything I should or shouldn't be doing?" Marjorie's stubborn streak kicked in again.

The lips tried once more to pucker, but couldn't beat whatever substance had been injected into them, resulting in what Marjorie could only interpret as a pout. "Take gentle exercise until you start your programme tomorrow. Don't overdo it, though."

"Like trying to touch my toes." Marjorie couldn't resist a dig, but added a chuckle to pretend she was joking.

Hannah met her attempt at humour with a stern response. "I must have a benchmark. You'll have to trust me to do my job. Look... Try not to worry, we're very good at what we do here. My assistant will have you walking without that stick in no time."

"Oh, that would be miraculous," said Marjorie. "I would so much rather walk without it. Can I begin now?"

Hannah shook her head. "Not until we've rebuilt your confidence. It doesn't pay to run before you can walk."

And yet one should be able to touch one's toes. Marjorie felt the irony. Now, she needed to get on with her investigation so that her miraculous recovery could come quickly.

Checking her watch to ensure Hannah had given her the full forty-five minutes, she said, "Thank you. I look forward to getting on with things tomorrow, then."

"Mm." Hannah strode to the door and opened it. Seeing Pete outside, she tried a smile and added, with a forced air of enthusiasm, "I look forward to seeing you tomorrow, Lady Snellthorpe. I'll be overseeing your care."

Yippee, Marjorie thought. A minute ago it was being handed off to a minion.

"And I look forward to seeing you too" – *as much as I'd look forward to having a tooth extraction* went unsaid – "except I thought you told me one of your assistants would work with me tomorrow."

"You must have been mistaken. I oversee all therapy sessions for newcomers, Lady Snellthorpe."

Not insisting the woman call her Marjorie like she normally would, she nodded. Marjorie noticed Pete giving Hannah an odd look and wondered what that was all about. Why was Hannah lying?

NINE

"Well? What did you find out?" Edna's voice cut through the air with a sharpness that made Frederick flinch. He had barely stepped into the hall before she was demanding answers.

Feeling a small twinge of annoyance at her impatience, Frederick took some deep breaths before replying. "We didn't have a lot of time to make much progress. Marjorie was busy paying fees for the first half hour; after that, a nurse gave us a tour. When that was finished, it was time for lunch."

"The place is impressive, isn't it?" Horace said, his eyes shining with enthusiasm.

"There's a lot there, if that's what you mean, but I didn't take to it."

Edna huffed. "You're just an inverted snob. It's a retirement palace."

"Where people are being knocked off, if you're proven right."

"Come on, you two, let's not argue," Horace interjected. "We're a team, remember."

Frederick hung his coat on the coat rack, and they all moved into Edna's lounge where a pot of tea and three cups were waiting.

"The chap that showed us around, Pete Grabham, was pleasant enough," he said as Horace poured. "The administrator came across as cold."

"Yeah, Pete's a good sort," Edna concurred.

Horace leaned forward. "Other than not taking to the place, Fred, did you get any inkling that something might be wrong?"

"Not really. Pete was initially open with regards to a couple of former residents complaining about a lack of activities and suchlike, but once he had to tell us they were dead, he clammed up. Marjorie tried to get some information out of the administrator, Ruby Haigh, by pretending to be a friend of a friend of Jackie Bagshaw."

Horace chuckled, stroking his chin thoughtfully. "Clever tactic. How did Ruby react?"

"She broke the news about the woman's death as though it was an everyday occurrence with no empathy whatsoever. But when it came to business, her manner was one of efficiency and sharpness. I've no doubt that she's a capable administrator."

Horace gave Edna an enquiring look, but she said nothing, so he carried on. "It doesn't tell us much. I had a few dealings with Ruby, and as you say, she's businesslike. I don't suppose she's paid to care and I'm sure the staff must all get used to people dying."

"Maybe. But she didn't have to come across as so cold-hearted. Pete, on the other hand, seemed genuinely sad about the residents' deaths."

"He's caring, is Pete. When I visited Edna, I got the impression he had little time for Ruby Haigh."

"Nobody likes her. She's all about money," said Edna.

"She seemed pleasant enough to me," said Horace.

"That's because you're a flirt, Horace Tyler," teased Edna.

"And you were giving her money," she quipped with a knowing smirk.

Frederick had wondered how Edna had afforded the fees for such a place. Horace had not only recommended it, but had also paid for it. He really was a puzzle at times.

"We met Apollo. You should have told us where his cage was. He nearly gave us away."

Edna's hand flew to her mouth. "Sorry, I forgot. He's Ruby's eyes and ears. I'm sure that's why she keeps him so close to her office. Lots of things are said in that waiting area and I've a feeling she takes notes. Was her door open?"

"No, she closed it after leaving us waiting for our tour. We saw the resident cat."

"Timmy. I bet he was lying on someone's lap in the warmest sitting room."

Frederick grinned. "Indeed, he was. Pete said one of the apartment residents used to feed him. Was that Jackie?"

"Yes. She loved him like he was her own. Jackie had a thing for cats. I thought he was hers until Carl told me he had been given to the rehab centre for some reason."

"Pet therapy," said Frederick. "Apparently, the manager read an article on the topic, which might have been the same one I read about stroking pets lowering blood pressure."

Edna yawned. "I can see how that could work, but all that hair shedding. I wouldn't want to keep an animal."

Frederick looked around at the untidy room and inwardly agreed it wouldn't be a good idea.

"You got on well enough with Hercules last Christmas," said Horace.

"More like he got on with me," said Edna. "Wretched animal wouldn't leave me alone."

"Marjorie likes the grounds." Frederick refocused the conversation. "They are really impressive apart from the pond, which needs a good clean. Pete didn't seem that fond of the cold air, so we didn't get to explore beyond a short walk. One thing Marjorie wasn't happy about was being told she would be using the gym. She's got an appointment with the physio this afternoon."

Edna smirked. "Hannah McManus. Do you remember that notorious dirty wrestler back in the seventies?"

"Mick McManus," said Horace.

"By dirty, I assume you mean he cheated?"

"Oh yes, he made a career out of fouling, but I always suspected he put it on for show. His dirty tricks added entertainment value and all that, attracting boos from the crowd. Anyway, the reason I mentioned him is that it wouldn't surprise me if Hannah was from the same family. The residents refer to her as 'Hannah McMighty' because of her towering height and haughty attitude. Mark my words, our Marge will give her a run for her money in their physio session."

"Poor Marjorie," said Horace. "Will I get to meet the mighty Hannah?"

"Most of the new people do, but if you're lucky, not more than once. She carries out an initial" – Edna raised her fingers in air quotes – "assessment, more like a humiliation session, and then she passes the clients and their treatments on to her minions. I saw a physio assistant most of the time, as well as Diana Ferrett. She's got a heart of gold, that one."

"I think that's the woman who came to show Marjorie to her room after lunch. We briefly met one of the outside residents while we were with Ruby, and then two more for lunch."

Edna huffed, snapping impatiently, "Out with it, then. Who did you meet?"

"A hypochondriac fellow – at least, that's what Marjorie concluded, and the administrator gave the impression he was not as ill as he made out."

"Darren Butler," said Edna. "He's always complaining he's

suffering from a worse illness than anyone else has ever had, and he tells everyone how the doctors say he's a walking miracle."

Frederick smiled. "That's the one. I take it you met him too."

Edna rolled her eyes. "I made the mistake of asking, 'How are you?' on the first day."

"And instead of answering fine, like the rest of us would, he told you how poorly he was."

"Didn't he just," said Edna, raising her eyebrows. "Most people run in the opposite direction when they see him coming, but I felt sorry for him. He's lonely."

"Pete told us about an ex-detective inspector we noticed during the tour. A man called Victor Redman. Marjorie was keen to speak to him, so we had lunch with him and a former journalist, Isabelle Stoppard. She's incredible, I can't believe she's ninety."

"I didn't know there was an ex-detective living there." Edna's face formed a frown.

"I'm surprised. You can't miss him; he prowls around like he's looking for someone to arrest. I don't think he'd be good on a stakeout, he seems far too agitated."

"I know the man you mean," said Horace. "The chap with Parkinson's."

Frederick nodded.

"How come I didn't meet him if you did?" Edna snapped at Horace.

"Remember, you were quite frail when you first went into the home for rehab. Once you were on the mend, you spent most of your time with your musician friends, and when you weren't with them, you were having treatment, or I was visiting. I spoke to the chap a couple of times while I was waiting for you, but he didn't tell me he was an ex-detective. He was a gruff sort."

"He comes across like that, but I think he's got a softer side.

Isabelle implied he resents not being in charge. It must be hard being in a place like that when you've given orders your whole life. He—"

"And who's Isabelle?" Edna was becoming more and more impatient, and Frederick wasn't good at handling her. It was Horace who replied.

"Fred just told us she's a retired journalist who he and Marjorie had lunch with. You need to listen, Edna." Frederick was glad it was Horace who'd said what he was thinking. If he'd said it, she'd have torn him to shreds.

"Oh, her. She was too toffee-nosed for me, hardly ever spoke."

Frederick wanted to point out how friendly Isabelle had been with him and Marjorie, and how compassionate and thoughtful she'd been when Victor struggled with his soft diet, but he didn't want to rile Edna.

"You were about to say something else about Victor." Horace poured Frederick and Edna a fresh cup of tea.

"Just that he implied there was something odd going on at the home and that Marjorie should be careful."

Horace raised his eyebrows. "Did he go into details?"

Frederick shrugged. "No."

"Well, didn't you ask him?" Edna sounded harsh, but looked concerned.

"I'm sure Marjorie would have, but that's when Isabelle joined us and she told him to stop with his conspiracy theories. There's probably nothing to it."

"That's as may be, but if a retired detective thinks Marjorie should be careful, I'm not happy to leave her in there by herself. Time for me to get on with things." Horace got up and marched out to the hall. A few minutes later, they heard the front door closing.

"Where's he gone?" Frederick asked.

"To meet a London train. That Harley Street doctor friend

of his has already emailed the letter he needs, but they couldn't expect a pharmacist to dispense a false prescription, so he did it himself. Rather than use a courier, Horace asked a conductor friend to bring it up."

Frederick shook his head. "How does he know all these people?"

"He used to travel a lot – still does. He's always telling me to be nice to people because you never know when you might need them. I guess this is one of those people he's been nice to and one of those times."

Frederick knew that Edna's heart was in the right place, but she wasn't always nice to people, especially to him. He looked around her sitting room again, noticing how dusty it was. It couldn't be helping her breathing, sitting in this room. He made a mental note to ask Horace to suggest a cleaner.

"I'll do the dishes," he said. "Would you like some more tea?"

"I'd rather have coffee. It was Horace who fancied tea."

"Coffee it is, then." Frederick found his way to the kitchen and his heart sank at the sight.

TEN

The autumn leaves crunched under Marjorie's feet as she meandered along the garden path. The flowerbeds contained a few hardy chrysanthemums, pansies, and winter flowering roses. She continued her stroll and came across an empty bowling green. Although it was not in use because of a spell of recent cold weather, she had no doubt it would be popular in the summer. Bowling was a pastime she and Ralph had considered for after he retired, but somehow he never did quite retire and they hadn't found the time.

The sunlight was fading behind dark clouds and Marjorie felt a sudden chill run down her spine, along with a feeling she was being watched. She paused, listening intently. There was nothing but the sound of rustling leaves. Yet the hairs on the back of her neck stood on end. She turned sharply, peering into the shadowy edges of the garden. Was that a flash of movement behind the hedgerow? No, surely it was just a trick of the light.

Marjorie pulled her coat tightly around herself and continued, picking up her pace ever so slightly. Another shiver shook through her and she once more glanced over her shoulder. The path behind lay empty, apart from stray leaves. Still, she couldn't shake the feeling of unseen eyes watching her.

Marjorie's heart pounded against her ribcage. She scolded herself for being so foolish. With the sun now completely hidden and the clouds threatening rain, she decided to head back inside. Every so often, she stopped, imagining she was hearing somebody behind her.

Eventually, she shook her head, muttering to herself, "Get a grip, Snellthorpe. Edna's got you rattled."

When she arrived at the large turning circle, Marjorie glanced around and saw Victor staring out from his window. She waved, but he didn't wave back. He seemed absorbed in his own world. Poor man had a lot to contend with. Marjorie took one more look behind her and heaved a sigh of relief when she saw Timmy chasing a few leaves.

"So, it was you out there," she said, laughing at her foolishness. She shrugged her shoulders and wandered indoors, remembering to slow down and use her cane.

Diana Ferrett, the care assistant, ran to greet her, a frown on her face.

"There you are, Lady Marjorie. I've been looking everywhere for you; I was getting worried."

Marjorie straightened her posture, defiant. "There was no need. I simply went for a stroll around the gardens. A little fresh air hurt no-one. And as you can see, I had company."

Diana moved aside to allow Timmy back inside, clicking her tongue. "Hannah's care plan says you can't go outside unaccompanied until she clears you."

"Humph! And what's Hannah going to do about it? Lock me up? I don't need anyone's permission to take a walk."

Diana forced a laugh. "I wouldn't challenge her if I were you. I'm sure it's for your own safety. And I'd rather not get into trouble." Marjorie sensed fear in the young carer's hazel eyes.

"I wouldn't want to get you into trouble, Diana, so I'll

behave. It just seemed a lovely afternoon for a walk and I love the changing colours at this time of year. Hannah didn't tell me I needed an escort to go outside, and I was feeling so much more confident after my session with her, I just couldn't help myself."

Diana had a kind smile and appeared generally unassuming. "No harm done." She pointed Marjorie towards a plush armchair in the sitting room. "Why don't you take a seat and I'll fetch some tea to warm you up?"

Marjorie thanked her, but huffed as she sank into the chair. She realised there was no point arguing with Diana against Hannah's rules. Nevertheless, she had no intention of becoming a prisoner in this place. The fresh air called to her, and she would not be kept indoors for long. At least she could rest assured Diana wouldn't mention her escape to the overbearing Hannah McManus.

Apollo, however, wasn't so forgiving. She could hear the mischievous bird squawking, "WHERE'S MARJORIE? WHERE'S MARJORIE? SHOULDN'T BE OUT."

Diana reappeared with tea and biscuits and laid them on a table next to her. "Ignore Apollo. He'll forget about it in no time and Hannah's in her office. Ruby said he was going on about calling the police even before I asked her if she'd seen you."

"Why ever would he want to call the police? Or rather, want someone to call the police?" Marjorie wondered if Apollo really did have a sixth sense.

"Now you mention it, I don't know. He repeats things, which can go back to what he heard months ago, just to keep himself amused. If he were human, I'd swear he was out to cause trouble. Anyway, I'd better get on and help Pete with the medicines. Hopefully, I'll be a nurse myself one day soon."

"You'll make an excellent nurse," said Marjorie.

"Thank you." Diana hurried away until all Marjorie could see was the long chestnut-brown ponytail swaying from side to side.

Marjorie took a sip of tea. She had no intention of being chaperoned around like a senile old woman, but Diana didn't need to know any of that. When she looked up again, Darren Butler was rolling up in his wheelchair, a crocheted blanket spread across his lap.

"Afternoon."

"Good afternoon."

"She hunted you down, then?"

"If you mean Diana, yes. I went for a walk."

"Lovely day for a walk."

Marjorie eyed him sharply, immediately suspicious. Had he been the one following her in the garden and not Timmy? She noticed damp leaves stuck in his chair tyres.

"Yes, it was until it looked like rain, although the clouds seem to be clearing again," she said looking through a window. "Have you been out yourself?"

"Only to and from my apartment, it's not safe out there. You should be careful, walking outside on your own. You could fall over and freeze to death before anyone knew you were out there."

"Except Diana would have found me, wouldn't she?" Was Darren always so pessimistic, or was this some sort of veiled warning?

"This time maybe. But what about the next time? I had a fall once... broke my hip. The surgeon said it was the worst fracture he'd ever come across and I was lucky to be alive. Still got the metal inside to prove it. If it were warmer in here, I'd show you the scar, but they never put the heating on. I had hypothermia once..."

Darren launched into a litany of his health woes, from his lumbago to his bunions. Marjorie nodded along absently, watching as he fidgeted with the fringe of his blanket.

"... it's always freezing in here, that's why I wear my coat most of the time."

Marjorie's attention drifted back to what Darren was saying, and she thanked her lucky stars that the home didn't turn the heating any higher. It was stifling enough as it was.

"You'd better find Pete and get your medication, Darren," Cook called as she walked towards the kitchen.

"Is it that time already? I'd better go. The doctor says if I don't take my pills, I'll end up back in hospital. I'll catch you later and tell you about my hernia."

I can't wait, thought Marjorie, watching Darren scurry off in his self-propelled wheelchair. She gave Cook a nod of gratitude before turning her attention to the comings and goings at the main entrance, as well as what was happening inside the home. Apollo had quietened down, but was chuntering away to himself in words that Marjorie couldn't hear from where she was sitting.

A few people were dozing in the wingback armchairs. Marjorie wasn't surprised and wondered why the heating was up so high. How Darren could feel cold, she didn't understand. Perhaps there was something wrong with the man, after all.

She hadn't spent long enough in her own room to check the temperature, but if she couldn't work out how to do it herself, she would ask Frederick later to make sure he turned the thermostat down. Gina always kept her rooms at home set at temperatures Marjorie was comfortable with. The only decision Marjorie had to make, which was challenging enough, was which rooms to heat.

Tiring of people-watching, Marjorie turned her eye to a newspaper on the side table. She reached for it, reading the headlines before scanning the obituaries. Marjorie's attention was piqued when she read Jackie Bagshaw's name. The brief paragraph read:

Much loved aunt of Keith, Mark and Mavis passed peacefully away at home...

Jackie had clearly lived in her apartment long enough for her family to consider it her home. Marjorie noted that the funeral was to be held at Stonefall Crematorium on Thursday with a request that donations, rather than flowers, be made to Poppy's Cat Rescue Centre. The late Jackie Bagshaw was obviously fond of cats. Marjorie would be interested to know whether she had been the one who'd fed Timmy before her demise and whether the leasehold residents were allowed pets.

Other questions buzzed around inside Marjorie's head. *What happens to the lease once a resident dies? Did Jackie die from natural causes? What about Carl?* She hadn't found out much about him yet.

Marjorie shook her head, forcing her brain to concentrate on the obituary. It might look odd if she attended the funeral, but it would be worth mentioning it to Edna in case she would like to go. Edna might be able to find out from one of the nephews or the niece their thoughts on the home, and whether they felt the circumstances of their aunt's death warranted a closer look. If anyone had a right to refer the death to the police, it would be them. Although that would be of no use once the cremation had taken place.

Oh, Edna. I hope this isn't an expensive waste of time.

Marjorie finished the last drop of tea and sat back. Her eyelids grew heavy as the tea's warmth seeped into her system. She sank deeper into the plush chair. The murmur of voices faded away. Marjorie's chin dropped to her chest, and she felt herself drifting, the newspaper slipping from her hands.

ELEVEN

The manic cackling from the woman's throat was terrifying. Marjorie found herself tied to a clunky piece of gymnasium equipment with Hannah McManus standing, hands on hips, demanding she reveal the real reason for staying at Evergreen Acres.

Marjorie jerked awake. She gasped, relieved it had been a dream, but then faced a chaotic scene playing out in the middle of the lounge. It made her wonder if she was still trapped in a strange nightmare.

"Mr Butler, Darren, please lower your voice, you're frightening the other residents." Pete was standing with legs apart in front of Darren's wheelchair, blocking his path from whoever he was trying to target.

"I'm telling you, I saw what I saw." Darren Butler's voice was a frenzied mix of anger and belligerence. A sudden screeching sound followed his words as he performed an impressive manoeuvre that wouldn't look out of place on a racetrack, swerving around Pete and accelerating across the room like a professional driver. Victor Redman twisted his body to dodge the wheelchair's path, his arms flailing in an uncoordinated effort to stop himself from being knocked down.

"Steady on," cried the wide-eyed Victor, holding his hands up in a placatory gesture.

Darren was having none of it. He glared up at the former detective from his wheelchair, gesturing wildly with clenched fists.

"Don't you *steady on* me! I saw you snooping around in the empty apartments. Why don't you tell them what you were up to, eh?"

A crowd was gathering from all parts of the care home as news of the altercation seemed to have spread amongst those staying. They watched silently, their faces a mixture of confusion and fear as they waited to see what would happen next.

Pete had caught up by this point and brought Darren's wayward wheelchair to a stop with a pull of the brakes, preventing Victor from being accidentally, or otherwise, run over. Victor looked around nervously at the many eyes upon him before turning back to face Darren, and then Pete. He took a deep breath before speaking in a measured tone.

"I don't know what he's talking about. The man's paranoid."

"Me? You need to look in the mirror, mate. You're the one who's always skulking around like you're some sort of Sherlock Holmes, trying to make everyone feel guilty. It wouldn't surprise me if you turned out to be a criminal pretending to be an ex-detective. Either way, you're no different from the rest of us decrepit has-beens."

Marjorie watched as Isabelle Stoppard stepped forward, her voice strong and confident. "Stop this at once, Darren. Victor's not well and deserves more respect. And I take it you speak for yourself, because I for one AM NOT a has-been."

A loud squawk emanated from the foyer. "HAS BEEN. HAS BEEN. DECREP HAS BEEN."

Marjorie chuckled quietly. Apollo clearly struggled to

master the three complicated syllables of decrepit. A few of the onlookers grinned at the parrot.

Isabelle's and Apollo's sudden interventions seemed to break the spell that had been cast over the room. That, and the dinner bell sounding, did the trick. The crowd dispersed slowly, each person whispering their own theories as to whether there was any truth to the story of Victor snooping around the empty apartments before making their way to their respective dining rooms. Victor seemed relieved, but shaken.

Marjorie, too, wanted to know exactly what Victor had been up to. But why were her thoughts jumbled and why did she feel so drowsy? She had been surprised to see other members of staff, including the intimidating Hannah McManus, standing on the periphery, observing the crazy scene play out. The incident had reminded Marjorie of children in a playground shouting 'fight' and gathering around to watch, then going back to play – or, in this case, going to eat – as soon as someone broke the fight up.

"I've got a headache," said Darren, looking down at his trembling hands. "The last time I had a headache like this..."

Nobody was listening. Isabelle took Victor's arm and whispered something to him as she guided him into the residents' dining room. Hannah glared after them while Diana approached Darren.

"Come on, Darren. Why don't you have dinner in your apartment tonight? I'll bring it to you and you can take a couple of paracetamol for your headache."

Darren nodded, suddenly looking as ill as he claimed to be. Pete gave Diana a nod, then released the brake. Diana pushed the chair through the exit and out of the care home, but not before sending an admiring gaze back to Pete.

Hannah shot another general glower around the room, then marched to the office, coming out seconds later wearing a woollen coat and thick fur-lined boots. She flew out of the door, almost knocking someone over in her wake.

Thank heavens. Marjorie felt calm and joy in equal measure when she noticed that the man who had nearly suffered from Hannah's wrath was Horace. With suitcase in hand and a plastic eyepatch taped over his left eye, he strolled in followed by Edna. They walked towards the office, where Ruby was still standing, tight-lipped in the doorway after the fracas.

Marjorie ignored the wink from Edna lest Apollo had the ability to interpret the gesture and screech it from his perch. With a quick glance over at the parrot, she saw she needn't have worried. He was concentrating on his dinner, just like the rest of the residents. She still felt oddly drowsy, but forced herself up from her chair and into the same dining room where she'd eaten lunch. Victor and Isabelle were engaged in a whispered conversation, but Isabelle welcomed her when she headed their way.

"Join us," she said.

"Thank you." Marjorie perched herself on a dining chair and offered Victor an encouraging smile.

He was visibly shaken. "Sorry about all that. We rarely get that kind of behaviour in here."

"From where I was sitting, it's not you who needs to apologise," Marjorie replied.

"Indeed not. I don't know what got into Darren, though. He's never behaved like that before," Isabelle offered.

"He used to behave like it a lot," said Victor.

Isabelle turned her head, open-mouthed. "You never said you knew Darren before you came here."

"It's not something I talk about." Victor tapped his nose. "Especially to gossiping women."

Isabelle had the decency to laugh. "You're really something, Victor Redman. If you have a history with the man, presumably from your line of work, you could at least have warned me."

"I knew him when he was a lot younger. Before today, I didn't realise he remembered me, but after that exhibition, I guess he does. He's not changed a bit."

"And he bears a grudge," added Isabelle.

"Maybe."

Cook arrived at the table to show Marjorie the menu.

"I'm not that hungry," Marjorie said. "Might I just have a little pasta?"

"Of course you can. You look worn out. Has it been a long day?"

"I do feel unusually tired."

Marjorie noticed a glance exchanged between Victor and Isabelle.

Once Cook had left, she asked, "What was that all about? Do you know something I don't?"

Isabelle checked over her shoulder before speaking. "Victor has a theory that staff put sleeping draughts in the tea sometimes. Personally, I don't concur, it makes no sense. I think it's the heat."

"It is stifling in the sitting rooms despite the doors being open. I keep my windows open at home, at least for part of the day."

"There you are, that explains it," said Isabelle.

"Have it your way," said Victor. "I'm telling you there are strange goings-on in this place."

Marjorie took the opening. "Is that why you were in the empty apartments?"

"You're as sharp as you look," said Victor.

"Did you find anything?"

"That would be telling, wouldn't it? I'm not saying I was in those apartments, but if I was, I had good reason to be."

"Oh, Victor! You have to stop this nonsense." Isabelle turned to Marjorie. "As I said before, Victor can't quite believe that crimes aren't being committed or that people die naturally. Even when they're old."

"Old they might have been, but there was nothing wrong with them as far as I could see." Victor scowled at his pureed dinner as a carer placed it on the table. "Not like some of us. I'm surprised I'm not the one who's dead, living off this stuff."

"It's highly nutritious and you know it," argued Isabelle before turning to Marjorie. "We have this argument over every meal, but the dietician makes sure the food he's served is as good as yours or mine."

Victor turned his nose up. "You eat it, then. It still tastes like mush to me. If they don't get you one way, they'll get you another."

Isabelle sighed, her attention still on Marjorie. "Apart from the heat, how are you finding your stay?"

"So far, so good. I could do without the gymnasium work Hannah McManus has prescribed."

"We call her Hannah McMighty because she's above herself. Thankfully, I have nothing to do with her, but she sees Victor."

"And Darren," Victor said, defensively. "I'm not the only one who needs a bit of physio."

"It's a lovely place, though," said Marjorie.

"Other than when you're being drugged," Victor added. "Or listening to some ex-criminal losing the plot."

"I expect it was the heat that made me sleepy, but I grant you, the argument was a little disconcerting."

"I love your use of the English language, Marjorie. Truth is, even the leopards you think might have changed their spots, they never do."

Marjorie thought it might be worth another try. "You didn't say how Darren crossed your path."

Victor swallowed a spoonful of the pureed food, wincing as he did so. Then he looked at Marjorie and Isabelle.

"He murdered his mother-in-law – she was the one with money and Darren's wife inherited. He got away with it."

"Does that mean it wasn't proven?"

"I said you were sharp and you are, Marjorie. You'd have made a good detective. Yeah, you're right, we couldn't get enough proof to convince the CPS to take him to court."

"But surely if there wasn't enough proof—" Isabelle wasn't allowed to finish.

"Just because he was clever, it doesn't mean he didn't do it," Victor snapped. "Now look at him – he's a hypochondriac living in a mansion on the old woman's money."

"You believe he had something to do with the other residents' deaths, don't you?" Marjorie asked.

"Maybe I do, but just like before, I've got no proof. What I need to find is motive."

"And that's why you were in their apartments," said Marjorie. "No wonder he was so angry."

Isabelle stared in disbelief from one to the other. "You can't believe this nonsense, Marjorie, surely? Whatever his past, Darren has shown no aggression here before today. If he didn't kill his mother-in-law – and I trust the Crown Prosecution Service – perhaps he thinks you're going to accuse him of something he didn't do again, Victor."

"If you had any idea how many crooks get away with murder and other stuff, you wouldn't have as much trust in the CPS as you do. You're gullible, like the rest of society."

"But isn't it down to the police to find enough evidence to bring a case to court, and then for the courts to pass judgement?" Isabelle stood her ground.

"Aye. It is and we do our best, but when evidence is destroyed and idiots provide criminals with false alibis" – Victor dropped his spoon and stood up – "it ain't as easy as it looks on the telly. But this time, I'm gonna get him."

The two women watched Victor shuffle out of the dining room.

"I worry about him," said Isabelle. "This is just what he's been looking for, but if he's not careful, it will kill him."

Marjorie was thoughtful as she munched through the rest of her pasta. "What if he's right?" she said eventually.

Isabelle giggled, a nervous sound. "He's not right. Victor can't accept that he's no longer a policeman and, what's more, he bears grudges. I bet there are hordes of innocent people out there he swears are guilty. He's even told me about many accused who juries found not guilty, but he's convinced they got it wrong. I love the man dearly, but he's obsessive, and this obsession isn't good for him."

"You might be right," said Marjorie. "It does sound rather far-fetched that people are being murdered in a care home."

Isabelle nodded. "Exactly. It's a ridiculous thought."

"Especially in one as grand as this," Marjorie added.

TWELVE

"I hope you enjoy your stay as much as your friend Mrs Parkinton did." Ruby Haigh's voice was high and bubbly. She had a massive grin on her face, her eyes twinkling. She'd never been like that with Edna, but Horace had a way of winning over the most difficult people. And in Edna's view, Ruby Haigh fell into the difficult category.

"I'm sure I shall. Edna's not stopped singing your praises."

Ruby's eyebrows rose up her forehead, forming two perfect arches. Her puzzled eyes widened, waiting for Edna to respond. Edna's true feelings did an internal eye roll, but she was unable to perform a real one with Ruby staring at her.

Taking a deep breath in, she gritted her teeth, saying, "Everybody was so helpful, they got me back to feeling like myself again."

Ruby straightened, folding her hands. Her demeanour shifted back to the one of official self-importance that Edna was more familiar with. Through pursed lips, she acknowledged the reluctant praise.

"We're always happy to hear from former clients. Our aim is only to please. Now, Mr Tyler, a member of staff will remove your eye shield in the morning, and then they'll start to administer the drops as prescribed. If you wouldn't mind waiting outside, I'll let Senior Nurse Grabham know you're ready for a tour."

"I'm sure Pete's busy, what with dinners and all that," said Edna. "I can show Horace around. Just tell us which room he's in and I'll do it."

"Actually, I'll take you up on your kind offer, Mrs Parkinton. Senior Nurse Grabham is a little behind schedule. If you'd like to start in the dining room, there will be a dinner for you both. As for the room, you'll know it well. Mr Tyler is in your old room. Let a member of staff know if you need anything."

Normally, the stiff and starchy Ruby would have argued with Edna, but she had seemed unsettled when they arrived, and Edna suspected something had kicked off. They'd heard raised voices when they were getting Horace's case out of the car. Then Hannah McManus had come hurtling through the doors like a hurricane. Had Marge managed to stir up trouble already?

"Come with me, Horace. We'll get some food, and I'll give you a tour afterwards. He knows some of the layout from visiting me," she said to Ruby.

"Yes, of course," said Ruby. "If there's anything you need, Mr Tyler, you know where I am."

If Edna didn't know better, she'd have thought from the flush of the face and neck that the officious administrator was flirting.

"Thank you for your kindness," said Horace.

As soon as they closed the door, Edna muttered, "Any more of that and I'll throw up."

"I was only being polite," Horace said. "Jealousy doesn't become you."

Edna felt a slight growl in her throat before turning her back on Horace and popping a finger inside Apollo's cage. She winked at him.

"I hope you're behaving yourself."

"DECREP HAS-BEENS. HAS-BEENS," replied the magnificent parrot.

"I wonder what that's all about," said Horace once she joined him and they were out of earshot.

"I don't know, but I bet Marge has got something to do with it. Come on, I'm hungry."

Horace nodded at the man Edna now knew was an ex-DI as he left the dining room. Victor Redman's mind was obviously elsewhere as he avoided eye contact and didn't return the greeting. He headed towards the main doors, shaking his head and muttering to himself.

"There's Marjorie," whispered Horace. "Shall we *introduce* ourselves?"

Edna chuckled. "You bet."

They strolled over to Marge's table, which happened to be the only one with two vacant seats. Edna scrunched her nose up at a plate of horrible syrupy stuff occupying one of the set places on the table.

Horace spoke first. "Hello, I'm new here. Do you mind if we sit with you?"

"Not at all," said the journalist woman, Isabelle. "You were staying here recently, weren't you?" she was addressing Edna.

"Yeah. I was getting over pneumonia, but all better now." At that moment, she turned away, overcome by a coughing spasm.

"Well, almost, anyway." Horace patted her on the back. "She recommended the place to me. I've just had cataract surgery, so will spend a few days here. Edna wouldn't manage the drops I need without poking me in the eye."

Edna laughed. "He's right, my hands aren't as steady as they used to be."

"Welcome to Evergreen Acres. I'm Isabelle Stoppard and

this is Marjorie Snellthorpe. Marjorie arrived today as well, so she will tell you what it's like from a newcomer's perspective. I live in an apartment outside."

"Delighted to meet you both." Horace pulled a chair out for Edna while a member of the kitchen staff cleared the other place for him. "As I've already said, this is Edna, Edna Parkinton, and I'm Horace Tyler."

"I'm happy to meet you both," said Marge. Her eyelids seemed heavy and her eyes dull, which was unusual. Edna hoped she wasn't putting too much on her friend and wished she was staying in the home, too. She hated the thought of missing out while her friends got to do the investigating on her behalf. Still, it couldn't be helped.

During the next twenty minutes, Cook offered both Horace and Edna hot meals, and the four of them chatted easily while they ate. After they'd exchanged chitchat about their professional backgrounds, Isabelle seemed to latch on to Horace's interest in her and, much to Edna's disgust, was in no hurry to leave. He just didn't know when to stop, continually encouraging her to regale them with celebrity stories from her past. Edna would have enjoyed them too, if it weren't for her impatient desire to have a conversation with Marge.

When Isabelle finished one of her celebrity stories, Edna cut in. "I was telling Horace on the journey in, a couple of people I got to know here died recently. It really upset me because they seemed so healthy."

Edna had hit a nerve. A glance passed between Isabelle and Marge.

Marge picked up her cue. "We were just speaking about it before you arrived. I don't know the people involved, but a friend of Isabelle's is concerned about the deaths. He used to be a detective."

"And I was explaining to Marjorie that Victor – ex-DI Redman – can't seem to accept the fact he's no longer a policeman and tries to invent situations that might exercise the analytical side of his brain. You might already be aware, they were both examined by the GP, Dr Branson, who visits the home, and both died of natural causes."

"That's what I was told as well," said Edna. "But don't you think it strange they were stirring up trouble and, soon after, both died suddenly?"

"So, what's the alternative? That a member of staff is killing people? If you believe that, I'm afraid you'll be on a different path to Victor. He suspects a resident."

Horace patted Edna's upper arm. "Edna likes to think she's a bit of a sleuth in her spare time. I've been trying to convince her to accept the doctor's conclusion, that her friends died naturally. It's better to go suddenly than linger on for months, or years."

"It wouldn't surprise me if that's what's getting to Victor," said Isabelle. "He's got Parkinson's disease and is on the decline, although he's still got all his faculties and the medication he takes is keeping him as well as can be expected."

"Is Victor the man we passed when we came in?" Horace asked. "He looked like he had a lot on his mind."

"He has," said Isabelle, looking at Marge.

"I've had cancer," said Edna, "so I know what it's like living with uncertainty."

"But you're clear at the moment," said Horace, looking suddenly concerned.

"That isn't what's worrying Victor right now. I expect you'll hear about it soon enough, but one of the residents, Darren Butler, had a shouting match with Victor just before dinner."

"Darren?" Edna felt her jaw drop. "The hypochondriac Darren?"

"Yes."

"I thought he was a harmless sort," said Edna. "Annoying, but—"

"So did I until I witnessed the unpleasant outburst. Then I found out—"

"Found out what?" Edna asked.

"I'd rather not say. I hate gossip."

"You said you were a journalist." Edna's hand went to her mouth. She had spoken without thinking. Marge shot her a warning glance.

Isabelle's eyes narrowed, before softening. Sighing, she said, "I interviewed celebrities for a living, but I published factual stories. My articles were never gossip, although Victor would agree with you."

Edna wasn't giving up that easily. "You still haven't said what you found out about Darren."

"Nor will I. If you'll excuse me, it's time for me to retire."

Horace stood and moved to pull Isabelle's chair back for her. "It was a pleasure speaking with you. I hope we get to chat some more."

Isabelle glanced warily towards Edna before saying, "I hope so too. Goodnight."

The dining room had long since cleared, but there were still a few kitchen staff milling around, cleaning tables.

Horace eyed Edna. "Is there anywhere we can relax?"

"I know just the place," said Edna. "Follow me."

Edna loved seeing the look on Horace and Marge's faces when she walked them around the outside of the building to the onsite bar.

"You never mentioned this place," said Horace.

"Didn't I?" She feigned a look of innocence. "The apartment residents and staff use it most, but Jackie showed me where it is. It's often empty at this time of night during the week, but there is usually a quiz at the weekend. This is where we played a few songs." Edna felt a churning in her stomach as emotion rose to her throat.

"Pete didn't include this in my tour," said Marge. "Will Frederick be able to find us?"

"Oh, I forgot to tell you. He said that because Horace came in a day early and we would see you tonight, he'd do some research on the home." Edna noticed a look of disappointment in Marge's eyes. She might pretend she wasn't that close to Fred, but Edna knew differently. "He said to tell you he'll be here in the morning," she added.

Horace took charge of pouring drinks and placing money in the honesty box that was chained to the bar. They had the building to themselves for now and needed to take advantage of the opportunity.

Even with a glass of brandy in her hand, Marge didn't look right.

"Are you okay, Marge?"

"I'm not sure. I believe it might have been the tea."

Edna's heart sank. Was her friend losing her marbles?

"You'd better give us a bit more information than that."

THIRTEEN

Marjorie's mind was a jumbled mess, making it impossible for her to accurately express her emotions. It was as if her thoughts were shrouded in a dense fog, one minute clear and the next distorted and hazy. She gazed up at her friends, their expressions mirroring her own confusion and concern.

Victor's words still echoed in her mind, causing a knot to form around her heart, making it difficult to breathe. Could what he said be true?

"I can't quite put my finger on it, but something just doesn't feel right since I fell asleep this afternoon. When I told Victor about dozing off, he mentioned something about staff giving people sleeping draughts without consent. It's absurd, I know, but I feel strange because I never nap during the day unless I've had a few drinks over lunch." Her words tumbled out in a jumble as she struggled to make sense of everything.

"Now you mention it, I nodded off a lot more when I was staying here than I usually do, but I put it down to boredom," said Edna.

"Isabelle said it was most likely the heat, which makes

sense," said Marjorie, realising just how paranoid she was sounding.

Her words seemed to trigger a reaction in Horace. His normally smooth brow creased into deep furrows.

"I doubt anyone in an establishment like this would resort to drugging their clients. I agree with Isabelle and you. It must have been the heat. It hit me as soon as I walked in the door."

Edna huffed in annoyance, not happy with Horace's dismissal of her opinion. "Or maybe it was just the boredom, like I said," she interjected, crossing her arms.

"Quite," said Marjorie. "Most likely a combination of the two. We're not used to sitting around all day." Not that Marjorie had done a lot of sitting around since she arrived, but her agreement would help Edna to feel less threatened. "I don't think it will be necessary to organise an outing, Horace. The people here are talkative enough, so our time would be best spent getting to know Victor and finding out whether Darren is a killer, like our ex-detective thinks he is."

"Is that what Isabelle wouldn't tell us?"

"Yes, it was."

"We could still have an outing. I could ask if I can come along."

"Actually, I think you and Frederick can be of more use elsewhere." Marjorie watched Edna's face drop. Her lips pursed, and her expression turned as dark as the wig she was wearing. Marjorie was well aware of how Edna hated to miss out, but was pleased that her clarity of thinking seemed to be returning. The makeshift pub's temperature was much more comfortable than that inside the home.

After swirling the ice in her glass and taking a sip of her whisky, Edna fidgeted with her wig, something she did when under stress. Her eyes fixed on Marjorie's.

"Like where, Your Ladyship?"

"Now, now, Edna," said Horace. "Be nice."

"How about Jackie Bagshaw's funeral?"

"Oh."

"Before I fell asleep this afternoon, I browsed a local newspaper. Jackie's death was announced in the obituary section. The piece mentioned two nephews and a niece, along with the name of the crematorium. The funeral's the day after tomorrow."

Edna stroked her chin thoughtfully, her heavy foundation cracking. "Was it Stonefall Crem?"

Marjorie nodded.

"I could ask them what they thought about the home," said Edna.

"And more specifically, what is on the death certificate about how Jackie died," added Marjorie, her eyebrows knitting together.

"That's a good idea, Edna," said Horace, nodding in agreement. "Tackling the matter from many angles makes sense."

"But why does Fred need to come? He didn't know the woman," objected Edna.

"You can tell them he's come to support you in your grief, knowing how fond of Jackie you were," suggested Marjorie. "With three people to speak to, and two of you, it will allow you more time to gather what information you can."

"Maybe, but Fred? It's not like he's good with strangers, is it?"

"Give him a chance," urged Horace, placing a reassuring hand on Edna's arm. "He ran a successful pharmacy for fifty years, he must be able to speak to people. Just don't intimidate him."

Marjorie was pleased it was Horace advocating for Frederick rather than her, because Edna took the mild criticism in good humour.

She chortled. "Okay, point taken. He can talk to the nephews and I'll take the niece."

"Although we haven't asked him yet," Marjorie pointed out.

"Oh, never mind about that. He'll do what he's told."

"And that's not intimidating," murmured Marjorie. Even Horace didn't have an answer for Edna's nerve. He shrugged helplessly, then looked at Marjorie.

"What's our next move?"

"Apart from going to bed, I propose we speak to as many individuals as possible, starting tomorrow. That's if Sergeant Major McManus lets me out of the gymnasium."

"Hannah McMighty," said Edna.

Scrutinising her cousin-in-law, Marjorie added, "You didn't warn me about her. How did the two of you get along?"

"We didn't. She made it clear from the beginning she had no interest in me. Too busy trying to impress those with the most money. I overheard a conversation between two physio assistants – who were the ones she delegated to teach me breathing exercises. They were saying she's got problems at home. They also mentioned tension between her and Pete."

Marjorie recalled the non-verbal exchange between Pete and Hannah following her assessment. Edna's words confirmed what she had surmised.

"Did they mention what sort of problems she has at home?"

"Not that I remember. Can't say I was interested at the time. I didn't take to the woman and assumed if she had problems, they were most likely of her own doing. Though in hindsight..." She trailed off, finishing her drink and holding out the empty glass for Horace to refill.

"Sorry, old girl. Water for you, unless you plan on taking a taxi home."

Edna's forehead creased into a frown. "Oh, right. I wondered why there was only a smidgen of whisky in that glass. I forgot you're staying here and I'm driving back. Sparkling water with orange juice, then." Returning her attention to Marjorie while Horace poured her a drink, she said, "If

Hannah's a suspect, we ought to find out if these problems have any bearing on the investigation."

"I never would have thought of that."

Edna missed the sarcasm and replied, "That's why you've got me to help direct proceedings."

Marjorie sighed inwardly, but was soon cheered when Horace handed her a refilled glass of brandy. Edna scowled, but said nothing about it. Instead, she spoke to Horace.

"You'll have Diana under your spell in no time. She likes to talk, and she's about the friendliest person you'll meet in this place. See what she knows about it."

"Diana wants to be a nurse," said Marjorie. "Also, I have a sneaking suspicion she's got a crush on Pete."

"Really? I know about her wanting to be a nurse, but how did you find the other out? You've only been here a couple of hours."

Because I listen to people and observe, thought Marjorie, but she said, "It's just a hunch at the moment. Something about the way she looks at him."

"She might be cosying up to realise her ambition," Edna argued. "He's a lot older than her."

"Since when does age have anything to do with love?" With an eye for younger women, Horace would not think it was unusual.

"Younger women only want what they can get from older men... Take that smirk off your face, Horace Tyler, I mean money, and I doubt we're talking about love here."

Horace grinned. "Fair point. Although I doubt a senior nurse, even in a private facility like this, has the sort of money to satisfy a gold digger. If her crush isn't genuine, perhaps she feels he can help her with her ambitions. I'll tell her I have contacts—"

"You'll do no such thing," snapped Edna. "On second

thoughts, you'd better talk to Diana, Marge. Horace can try his charm on Hannah McManus."

"I like a challenge," said Horace. "But I doubt a physiotherapist has any interest in eye surgery."

"I should have been the one to have eye surgery," said Marjorie.

"Never mind, Marge. The exercise will do you good."

"If it was a member of staff who killed your friends, although that's still in question, who would your prime suspects be?" Marjorie quizzed.

"Pete Grabham's nice, but not as sincere as he makes out, and he's overly concerned with the home's reputation. I think that's why he doesn't rock the boat. Still, I don't see him as a killer." Edna stared into space for a while. "Until Jackie died, I wasn't really imagining anything strange was going on, and I wasn't well, so may not have been as astute as I normally am."

Marjorie felt Horace's eyes pleading with her not to comment. She didn't.

Edna continued. "The only fun I had was with my friends who played instruments or sang. None of them were professional like I was, but they were good. When I visit tomorrow, I'll drop in on Eleanor. She was the fourth person in our quartet and might have noticed something, although her memory's not the best. She's fine with singing and music, that's like muscle memory, but when it comes to what she did yesterday, there's not a lot there."

"That's disappointing, but worth a try," said Marjorie. "Does anyone else stand out?"

Edna shook her head. "I don't like Hannah, but like Pete, she doesn't strike me as a killer. More like someone a person would like to kill. Diana's too nice and Ruby is an unlikely candidate. They are the key players in the home, other staff come and go. I can't imagine any of them having a motive for wanting to kill people. Maybe I've got this all wrong. I wonder if we should just forget about it."

Marjorie was aghast. "Horace and I have booked in and paid for four days' care, we might as well see what we can discover. Victor Redman is on to something, of that I'm sure. I'd like to speak to him alone."

"Marjorie's right," said Horace. "Jackie's death really shook you up yesterday, Edna, and judging by what Marjorie said about this Darren fellow, I'd say you're on to something, too. Perhaps it's the residents we should look at if that's what Victor thinks."

Edna's shoulders relaxed as she sought reassurance. "Do you think I'm right?"

"You were right when you followed me and saved me from a psychopath on that river cruise, so I think we should persevere for now," said Marjorie. "And we should keep an open mind about whether it's a member of staff or a long-stay resident."

Edna brightened up immediately. "You're right. Thanks, Marge. Sounds like Darren Butler is a candidate, although he wouldn't have been top of my list."

"People can surprise you. He was furious with Victor this afternoon."

"Why?" Horace asked.

"He'd seen him in the empty apartments, and what's more, Victor believes he got away with murdering his mother-in-law in the past. Isabelle thinks that's just a case of Victor's dogged determination and inability to believe he could ever arrest the wrong person."

Horace drained his glass. "What about you?"

Marjorie shook her head. "Either theory could be the truth. We just need to find out which."

"Promise me you'll be careful. I wouldn't want anything to happen to either of you," said Edna. "Now I'd better be going before they send out a search party for you. They'll have taken your bags to your room, Horace. It's number 28 on the second floor. If you need a tour, I can give you one tomorrow."

"Thank you."

"Edna's right, we'd better get back. Diana has already warned me not to leave the home unaccompanied until the sergeant major, Hannah McMighty, gives me a pass," Marjorie said, chuckling.

"Strictly speaking, you're not unaccompanied," said Horace.

"I'm not sure a one-eyed man will count," said Edna.

"Well, it will remain my argument if challenged. Edna, would you ask Frederick to bring me a flask tomorrow when he visits?" asked Marjorie.

"Why would you want a flask? This place has everything."

"Just in case there's any truth in what Victor says, I'd like the option of drinking what I've prepared, although I expect I'll feel differently about it in the morning."

Edna rolled her eyes, but nodded. "Fine. But I'm not sure how much notice we should take of what that geezer says. He sounds weird to me."

"I would still like to have a decent conversation with him."

The three of them left the bar together. Marjorie noticed a face peering from the window of the nearest apartment. It was the same face that had been staring out when she came back from her walk: Victor Redman's.

Until tomorrow, Victor, she said silently.

FOURTEEN

The house was pleasantly quiet after Edna and Horace left for the care home. Frederick let out a contented sigh, grateful for the solitude. But at the same time, a slight ache tugged at his heart at the thought of not being able to visit Marjorie. He was worried about her. Still, he found solace in knowing that Horace had gone into the home a day early to make sure she was safe. And truthfully, he welcomed the opportunity to have some time alone. Despite the close bond the four friends had formed over the past few years, he still found Edna challenging at times, especially when Marjorie wasn't around to keep her in check.

The kitchen remained in disarray, with dishes piled up in the sink, and pots and pans strewn across the table. Despite Frederick's earlier attempt at tidying the cluttered space while Horace was out, it felt chaotic. Horace had returned with his pretend eye drops and had printed off the dubious letter from his Harley Street doctor friend. He had boasted as though he had just won the lottery, but Frederick could never embrace the thrill of these investigations like the others did. It made him feel like he would always be on the fringes. However, one thing he excelled at was research, and that's how he intended to spend this evening once he had restored order.

Frederick couldn't concentrate while the kitchen was in such a state, and he spent the next couple of hours tackling the pots and pans. He knew that Edna's recent illness was the most likely reason behind the mess, but he couldn't understand why she refused to hire a cleaner, even though Horace had told him he'd offered to pay for one.

Frederick disagreed with Horace in that he didn't feel leaving things as they were was the best way to deal with her reluctance. Horace was convinced Edna would see sense when the chaos became overwhelming. Whoever was right, Frederick couldn't stay in this house with the kitchen in a mess.

Once he'd finished, he stood back, admiring the gleaming surfaces, and wondered whether it would offend Edna that he'd taken things into his own hands. If it was a choice between her taking offence or preparing food and drinks in a rubbish tip, he'd deal with her wrath.

Not that anybody would prepare food for a while as the cupboards were bare, and he'd tossed everything except for the bottle of fresh milk in the dustbin because it was stale, mouldy, or out of date. If Edna was determined to resist employing a cleaner, at least she could start from scratch now her health was improving. Marjorie had assured him that Edna was usually a clean, if not tidy, person.

Frederick opened his laptop, but his stomach was grumbling, and he regretted only having soup at lunchtime. If the truth be told, the prestigious home had overwhelmed him, along with the reasons for Marjorie being there. He closed the laptop again and packed it into its case, donned his coat and left the house, heading to the local pub where they'd eaten the night before.

Unlike Edna's house, the pub was warm and welcoming, and the aromas were appetising. Frederick bought a pint at the bar and ordered a steak dinner, then headed over to a quiet table for two nestled in a far corner. He sipped his pint, imagining Marjorie sitting in the other chair and them having a cosy chat about anything other than murder. Although convinced Edna was imagining things, Frederick would do his duty and carry out some research.

"There you go, mate. Can I get you anything else?" The barman placed his dinner down on the table.

Frederick looked at the appetising steak. "Some English mustard and ketchup, please."

Once the additional condiments were in front of him, Frederick enjoyed a leisurely meal, hoping Marjorie was okay and that she wouldn't stay away for the full four days.

A smartly dressed man interrupted his reverie. "Excuse me, mate, is that chair taken?"

"No, feel free to move it."

"Cheers, mate." The man carried the chair to a nearby table where his family of five was ordering dinner.

After the barman cleared his table, Frederick opened his laptop, pleased there was free Wi-Fi. The pub was busy, but there were spare tables on the other side where the noisier punters gathered. He should be able to get enough work done without bothering anyone.

His first task was to do an online food shop for Edna. He could explain that it was part-payment for her putting him up. He opted for a delivery between eight and nine in the morning, so he could make sure he was up and dressed in time to receive it before going to see Marjorie.

Satisfied he and Edna would at least have some food options in the house, he could finally concentrate on the task at hand. He began tapping keys, starting with the home, and it didn't take him long to find who owned it and who had any financial interest in the elaborate concern. The rehab side of the business was set up as a privately funded centre which rarely took local-authority-funded clients, and when it did, there was a huge top-up fee that either the council or relatives had to fund.

Frederick dug deep into the fees, top-ups and extras that were available for purchase. As well as Horace's friend, other co-owners were a Dr Stephanie Branson and her husband, Miles Branson, who was the chief executive. Dr Branson was treasurer.

A quick delve into the finances via Companies House made Frederick frown. He was so engrossed in his research, he didn't see the person standing over him until she spoke and made him jump.

"I thought I'd find you in here."

Frederick looked up to see Edna holding a glass of whisky.

"I meant to leave a note." He fetched her a chair from the other side of the pub and found her staring at his computer when he got back.

"What's going on there?" She nodded to the screen.

"I'm not sure, but they seem to be sitting on a gold mine. There's so much money in the business, they could almost list it on the stock exchange."

"Maybe they want to expand," she said, not moving out of his seat.

Sighing, Frederick sat in the chair he'd brought along while Edna continued scrolling through the accounts he'd been scrutinising. She whistled.

"With what they charge, I'm not surprised they're rolling in it. I knew it was expensive, but had no idea how exorbitant it was until Horace paid the bill for his stay. No wonder he never let me see a price list or I'd have refused to go."

"He cares about you and he can afford it," said Frederick, unable to keep a slight resentment from his voice. Frederick himself was perfectly well set up, but compared to Horace and Marjorie, he felt poor. He could not keep up with Horace's lavish lifestyle, and yet Horace never made him feel inadequate.

Neither did Marjorie, but he'd like to be able to offer her something if their relationship ever moved beyond friendship. Not that there was any possibility it would; she'd made it clear she was only interested in friendship.

"Well?"

"Well, what?" Frederick saw Edna glaring at him.

She waved a hand in front of his eyes. "Wakey-wakey, you were in a trance. I asked what else you found out."

"Not much, I've not long started. I was a bit late coming here after..." He hesitated.

Edna sipped her whisky. "Thanks for tidying the kitchen. I would have got around to it, but I've been preoccupied."

At least he wasn't in the doghouse, which was a bonus. "I've also ordered a bit of a food shop to arrive in the morning. I hope you don't mind?"

"Point taken. I should look after my guests better." She folded her arms and glared around the pub.

"How's Marjorie?" he asked.

"She's doing all right, but was a bit drowsy. That detective chap, Victor, put the idea in her head she might have been drugged."

Frederick's heart skipped a beat. "What do you mean, drugged? How? Why?"

"Calm down. It's only his suspicion. As I said, Victor put it in her head. There was also an argument between the hypochondriac and the detective, but it was almost over by the time me and Horace got there."

Concern for Marjorie made Frederick's hands shake. "What about?"

"Darren – the hypochondriac – had seen Victor inside the empty apartments and got riled about it."

"What was he doing in the apartments?"

"Sniffing around. According to Marge, he suspects Darren of murder because the two have an unpleasant history. Something like that. Victor is convinced Darren got away with murdering his mother-in-law."

"And did he?" The thought of leaving Marjorie in that place had been concerning, now it was terrifying.

"Marge isn't sure. Victor's friend Isabelle says he's just not able to accept he can be wrong."

I know someone like that and they're sitting opposite me, thought Frederick.

"Don't worry. Marge says she'll be careful about what she drinks from now on. She wants you to take her a flask in the morning in case she decides to restrict her drinks to those she's prepared. I've got to do the same for Horace, but it's only a precaution and she'll have changed her mind by tomorrow, so don't get it out of proportion."

Frederick would have liked to remind Edna of how many times she got things out of proportion, but she was being unusually sympathetic, so he'd take the win.

"At least Horace is there and can keep an eye on her."

"Yeah, thoroughly enjoying himself, he is, too. By the way, the day after tomorrow, you and I are going to a funeral."

"Whose funeral?"

"My friend who died, Jackie Bagshaw. And before you try to get out of it, there's no point arguing. We're under orders from Marge. We've got to interview two nephews – that's on you – and a niece." Edna threw back the rest of her whisky. "You ready to go?"

Pulling his laptop away from Edna, he tapped a few more keys.

"I just need to check one more thing."

FIFTEEN

The soft mattress and plush bedding cradled Marjorie's tired body, but they were no match for her restless mind. She had spent the entire night tossing and turning, trying to make sense of all the information she had gathered since arriving at Evergreen Acres. As she replayed the events of her first day and the evidence – or lack of it – in her mind, doubts crept in about the validity of Edna's theory that two murders had taken place.

In the early hours, she'd pondered Victor's suggestion that her drink might have been spiked, but couldn't accept it. The first rays of morning sunlight brought with them the grasp of reason. It must have been the combination of a heavy lunch and heat that had caused her to fall into a heavy slumber. Marjorie had asked Horace to turn down the radiator in her room before she went to bed, so the lower temperature may have kept her awake. Yet even in the safety of daylight, faint doubts lingered like shadows in the recesses of her mind. Could someone have tampered with her drink, and if so, why? Was she truly safe in this place?

This would not do. She swung her feet over the edge of the bed.

"Be sensible, Marjorie, you're allowing the paranoid ramblings of a former detective who can't accept retirement to get into your head," she scoffed. After hastily washing and dressing, she made her way downstairs, determined to have a quiet word with Victor. She had to know whether he was living in the past, or whether he had observed something important that was worth considering. Marjorie also needed to know what he'd found in the empty apartments, if anything, that was likely to have any bearing on the prior residents' deaths.

Marjorie's plans were frustrated when she arrived in the dining room. Victor wasn't there, neither were any of the other apartment residents. A few people had taken seats in the larger dining room, but they, like her, weren't there long term. She knew where Victor's apartment was, having spied him gazing out of his window twice the day before, and debated with herself whether to pay him a visit.

"Good morning, Marjorie." Cook bustled around putting out menus for the day. "I hope you had a good night's sleep."

"It's always difficult to sleep in a strange bed," said Marjorie, deciding to take a seat.

"That's what I tell my Eric every time he insists we go away on holiday. I'd much rather stay at home these days. There's nowhere else I'd rather be, other than here, of course."

"You obviously enjoy your work."

"It's what keeps me going. I've always loved cooking and as I say to my Eric every day, it's more like a hobby than a job. He doesn't get it. Hates his job, my Eric does."

"What does your husband do?"

"He's an accountant. I don't know why he keeps on with it. He's moaned every day for twenty years, but still he trudges in, day after day. I suppose being a partner doesn't help. He can't just up and leave."

"Perhaps he likes it really," said Marjorie.

"Maybe. Some people aren't happy unless they're

complaining, and I have to admit my Eric's one of them. Still, he's a good husband and father. You might see him over the next day or two, he helps Ruby out with the books when she asks him to."

Marjorie's interest was piqued. "Oh? Doesn't the home have its own accountant?"

"That they do. Some fancy office in Leeds, but occasionally Ruby gets in a muddle, especially when the figures don't add up, and that's when she asks my Eric to step in before the bigwigs stick their oar in. It's not paid work, but Ruby's his cousin."

"Does he have to step in often?"

"More often than he should. Sloppy bookkeeping, my Eric calls it, but he usually manages to fix it for her."

Marjorie wondered what 'fix it' meant, but didn't like to suggest Cook's Eric was involved in anything underhand. Moving on to safer ground, she said, "I was hoping to see Victor this morning."

Cook checked her watch. "He'll be along any minute now. I can time my clock by him. He's never late. Five minutes after him, Isabelle will pitch up. It's like those two are dating and she always has to be respectably late. They're not dating, of course."

"I understand, I'm from a similar generation where men must always be on time and women must arrive a few minutes afterwards. What about Darren, does he come in here for breakfast?"

"Darren usually has breakfast in his apartment along with a whole pile of pills, or so he tells me. I never know what to believe when it comes to Darren. In fact, most of those from the apartments sort themselves out, but I don't think Victor – or Isabelle, for that matter – have ever cooked a meal in their lives."

"Victor said as much about Isabelle sometime yesterday." Marjorie examined her own soft hands. She did little cooking herself these days, but she used to host dinners for up to thirty people, even if most of the cooking was carried out by others. Edna often teased her she wouldn't know one end of a pan from the other, and she might have a point.

"Good morning, Marjorie. How are you this morning?" Horace joined her at the same table where they had eaten the previous evening. It was remarkable how easily they had both taken to their subterfuge.

"I'm very well, thank you. Did you have a good night?"

"Slept like a log," he said. "I've just been for a walk around the grounds. The senior nurse – Pete, isn't it? He suggested I get some breakfast, and then he'll take this blasted patch off my eye. I can see through the plastic, but I feel like Long John Silver wearing it, plus the tape's irritating."

Cook chuckled. "I'll leave you two to get on, and I'd better get a move on myself. I'll be back out to see what you would like for breakfast in a few minutes." Cook checked her watch again, looking at the entrance as she walked away, her brow furrowed.

"Has she got something on her mind?" Horace asked.

"I don't think so. She seemed chirpy enough. Unless Victor's going to be late for the first time ever. Apparently, she can set her clock by his arrival."

Horace poured coffee from the hot pot already placed on the table, most likely in readiness for Victor, and tea for Marjorie. "He could be avoiding the guy who gave him trouble."

Marjorie didn't get the chance to explain what Cook had just said because Isabelle swept into the room, but stopped abruptly when she saw the empty space.

"Good morning." Isabelle's greeting sounded hollow. Her face was tense and her eyes darted anxiously as she scanned the room. Marjorie and Horace replied with their own polite good mornings.

"Isn't Victor here yet?" Isabelle's voice was as tense as her expression. Marjorie noticed how much older she seemed this morning, wearing less makeup than she had the day before.

Horace shook his head.

Marjorie broke the silence, trying to sound cheerful. "Cook was just saying he's usually here by now, along with a joke about his perfect timekeeping."

"I expect it was all that nonsense yesterday that's upset him." Isabelle glanced towards the door.

Tension rose in Marjorie's throat as she answered. "As Cook told me he's never late, do you think someone should check on him? I agree, he seemed rather upset last night." Marjorie didn't mention the blank stare she'd noticed when he was looking out of his window.

Isabelle seemed uncertain. "It is unusual, but Victor doesn't like fuss."

"That's it," said Horace, decisively. "Let's all go. Safety in numbers and all that. The most he can do is bawl us out for interfering and I've got broad shoulders."

Horace didn't have very broad shoulders, but Marjorie knew what he was inferring wasn't meant to be taken literally.

"All right," said Isabelle. "As long as you take the blame if he's angry."

Horace grinned. "Always happy to oblige a lady."

The three of them must have made a peculiar sight scurrying towards the door, especially as Horace brought his coffee mug along for the ride.

"Be careful you don't spill that or Ruby will give you a rollicking," warned Isabelle.

"I hate to waste excellent coffee. And don't worry about Ruby. I think I can handle her."

Marjorie rolled her eyes at Isabelle, stopping herself just in time from saying he wasn't half as bad as he made out. That's when she also remembered to slow her walking and use her cane. She and Horace followed Isabelle to the first apartment, next door to the pub where they had gathered the night before.

Isabelle tutted. "Why didn't I notice that before?"

"What?" Horace asked.

"The closed curtains. Victor's curtains are never closed."

Marjorie felt tension rising as she observed Isabelle's wide eyes.

Horace tried the handle of the door, but it was locked, so he knocked loudly. There was no reply.

"I've got a key. Give me a few minutes," said Isabelle, hurrying along the path.

Marjorie and Horace exchanged a worried glance. "Do you think something's happened to him?"

"Let's hope not." Horace bent down and squinted as he peered through the letterbox. "It's too dark in there. Can't see a thing, especially with only one unencumbered eye," he said. "Maybe he's having a lie in, he could have taken a sleeping pill."

Marjorie's heart sank at the reminder of how sleepy she had felt the day before. She hoped if Victor had taken something, it was of his own volition.

Isabelle came scurrying back from an apartment three doors down. "Here. You go in, he'll be furious with me if I do it." She handed the key to Horace.

Horace turned the key and pushed the door open, but it stopped after a couple of inches, held by a security chain.

"Blast! I should have known," he muttered. "Let me see if I can reach the light switch." Horace stretched his long arm through the gap in the doorway and used his right eye to peer into the hall. "It's no use. I can't see anything. Victor! My name's Horace. We're worried about you. Come to the door, please," Horace called, then stepped back. "You try," he said to Isabelle, but she was frozen to the spot.

Marjorie stepped forward and peeked through the gap. She saw a reflection in a mirror on the wall and gasped.

"You'd better get help," she said. "He's on the floor."

While Isabelle hurried back to the main building, Horace took four steps back before rushing the door with his shoulder.

SIXTEEN

Horace was kneeling over the scrunched-up form of Victor Redman when Diana came hurtling through the door, followed shortly afterwards by Pete.

"There's a pulse. It's faint, but I think he's alive," said Horace.

Pete quickly took charge, rechecking Horace's findings, and nodding. "There's an ambulance on the way." He opened a large heavy case and quickly attached a blood pressure cuff to Victor's upper arm, undid his shirt buttons and placed electrodes on his chest, connecting everything to a small machine. Marjorie recognised it as a mini version of the type of monitors found in hospitals. Soon the monitor was supplying blood pressure, pulse, oxygen level and heart readings.

Pete placed his ear over Victor's mouth, listening.

Diana shook her head. "It's bad, isn't it?"

"Yes," Pete replied glumly.

"Not another one." Tears filled Diana's eyes.

"He's not dead yet. There's not much in the way of breathing, I might need an airway," said Pete, lifting Victor's chin. Diana rifled through the first aid case and handed a piece of equipment to Pete, who was hooking a finger into Victor's mouth. He dislodged a large piece of meat. "Idiot," he muttered.

Pete appeared satisfied with his work as he asked Diana to help him move Victor on to his left side. Victor's breathing was still raspy, and he was unconscious.

"Is this how you found him?" Pete's question was aimed at Horace.

"Yes. Isabelle was worried because he was late for breakfast."

"It's a good job you came when you did."

Victor was still wearing the suit he'd had on yesterday during the altercation with Darren. While the two staff members concentrated on the monitor and Horace answered Pete's questions, Marjorie placed a hand on the crook of Isabelle's elbow and steered her away and into a scruffy sitting room. She pulled open the curtains to allow light in. The window overlooked the grounds.

Isabelle's face was pale and drawn, worry etching her features as she stared through the window. Marjorie could hear Pete and another member of staff she didn't recognise discussing things with Diana and Horace about the monitoring. She closed the door to drown out the noise before returning to the window.

"I should have seen his curtains weren't open when I passed. He never closes them. I didn't think to look."

Marjorie raised an eyebrow. "Aren't they closed at night?"

"Victor doesn't sleep well, and when he can't sleep, he watches the night sky." A nervous chuckle followed before Isabelle added, "Knowing him, he thinks he's a night watchman."

Marjorie forced a smile. "Indeed. I saw him standing at the window a few times yesterday. In fact, he was standing right here after I'd had a nightcap with Horace and his friend, Edna, last night in the bar next-door." Marjorie looked out of the window from every angle, taking in the vista that Victor found so interesting. The turning circle and entrance to the home were clearly visible, as were the paths leading into various parts of the grounds. Timmy was just heading inside following a morning forage. This window was ideal for spotting any curious goings-on, or for someone who was nosey.

She turned around. The sitting room was untidy with papers piled on a table next to an armchair.

"Does the room look the same as it always does?"

"I think so. Victor doesn't like people coming in here. When I visit, we go into the back room, which has patio doors leading into the garden. We all have private gardens," Isabelle explained. "When he's not staring out of the window, he's in his garden. I must admit to having a peep through the window when Victor first moved in. I don't think it's changed much."

Marjorie was about to look through the papers on the table when Isabelle shuddered. "We shouldn't be in here. He wouldn't like it."

Isabelle was twitchy, so Marjorie reluctantly conceded, but not before noticing a scuff mark on the carpet. She vowed to come back later.

As they re-entered the hallway, an ambulance siren sounded like it was getting closer and closer. Isabelle leaped into action, opening another door which most likely led into a bedroom.

"I'll pack him some things."

Marjorie was twisting her neck to take another peek at the scuff mark on the carpet when Horace joined her.

"Pete's told me we need to leave."

"Is there a door from the kitchen?"

"I assume so. Why?"

"Let's go that way."

Using the pretence of not wanting to impede the ambulance

crew, Marjorie asked Pete where the kitchen exit was. He pointed towards an open door.

"Through there."

Once in the kitchen, Marjorie paused.

"I'll close the door," said Horace.

"Good idea," said Marjorie, hearing a kerfuffle as the paramedics arrived. She tried the back door handle. "This isn't locked."

"Maybe he didn't get the chance to lock it before he collapsed," Horace suggested.

"Hmm. What's this?" Marjorie picked a plate up from the work surface.

"An empty plate."

Marjorie ran a finger over it, lifting it up for Horace to see. "You see this?"

"Grease," replied Horace.

"Precisely. Victor has a pureed diet. He mustn't eat solids. If I'm not mistaken, this is beef fat and contained whatever it was that Pete removed from Victor's throat." She put the plate under her nose and sniffed.

Horace did the same. "I'd say it is. Is that why Pete was annoyed? Do you think he choked?"

"Possibly. His colour suggested not much air had got into his lungs and that rasping sound when Pete removed the offending item wasn't pleasant."

"You noticed that too. I was just pleased he was alive. Pete dislodged another piece of meat from his throat when he was on his side, but said there might be more further down. Silly fellow. If he survives, he'll be a bit more careful in the future. So, nothing sinister, then? Just a man fed up with eating mush. I saw the plate they cleared away from the table last night and I can't say I blame him."

"Hmm."

"You're not convinced?"

"Have you seen the state of this apartment? It's a bachelor pad." She walked around, opening and closing cupboards. "These are empty apart from a carton of thickening powder for drinks – which I doubt he uses. I expect he breaks the rules with his tea and coffee... not to mention this." Marjorie was opening the final cupboard door and pulled out one from a stash of bottles of Guinness.

"So what you're saying is that someone cooked him a portion of beef and the idiot ate it?"

"It certainly wasn't cooked in here. This cooker looks as though it's never been switched on. Someone has tried to make it look like he was breaking with his diet. I don't believe Victor is that stupid. He complains about his diet, but he's the kind of man who follows rules."

"Unless he's snooping around dead people's empty apartments."

"Yes, but that was a part of his job. The point is, I believe someone disabled him somehow and covered their tracks by leaving this plate here, most likely forcing meat down his throat after he collapsed. There are signs they dragged him from his front room into the hall, I assume to make it look as though he choked and fell, or crawled there after finishing his contraband."

Horace rubbed his chin. "So Edna's right. There is something bad going on here."

"If I'm right, Victor Redman was getting too close to finding out who killed Carl and Jackie."

Marjorie closed the cupboard door just as Diana came into the kitchen. "Are you still here?" Her eyes narrowed as she spied the plate on the side. "What's that?"

"I think it's the plate that contained his unauthorised food," said Horace.

Diana ran a finger over it. "I'll let Pete know." She placed some empty wrappers in the bin. "I have to help him account for the equipment we used. He gets in trouble if anything goes missing."

"Have the paramedics gone?" Horace asked.

"Yes."

"In that case, we'll use the front door," said Marjorie. "I'd like some breakfast."

"I almost forgot," said Diana, "I've got an appointment card here for the tests Hannah's ordered. You'd better not be late."

Marjorie took the card, which listed an appointment for a DEXA scan, followed by some blood tests. Her jaw dropped at the prices listed on the information sheet that came with the card.

"Did Victor always leave his back door unlocked?" Horace asked.

"He was an ex-copper, so I doubt it," said Diana. "Why?"

"We found it unlocked, that was all."

"I guess he didn't get the chance to lock it. If only he'd obeyed the rules. This happens when you don't obey the rules."

"That's a bit harsh," said Marjorie.

"She's right, though," said Horace. "He wouldn't be on his way to hospital if he hadn't eaten that meat."

Marjorie took the hint. Until they knew who was responsible, even Diana should be kept in the dark.

"You make a good point. Now, I'd better see if I can placate the fearsome Hannah by attending these appointments. Even she should understand that one can't always keep to time when emergencies get in the way."

"I wouldn't bank on that," said Diana, chuckling. "Sorry to say, Ruby wants you to pop by the office to pay for those before you go. I'll tidy up in here and lock up. You go on."

"Thank you. If it wasn't for your and Pete's quick reactions, things might have been a lot worse."

Diana brushed back a stray piece of hair, preening. "Do you think so?"

"Absolutely," said Marjorie. "Now, I'd better be on my way."

"I hate to be a nuisance," said Horace, "but as Pete's busy, do you think you could remove this patch from my eye? The doctor said I only needed to wear it yesterday and overnight."

"I'll do it for you now." Diana went to the sink and washed her hands before gently removing the tape that was securing plastic eyepatch. "There you go," she said.

"Much obliged," said Horace. "We'll see you later."

While heading along the path, Marjorie kept an eye out for Isabelle, but couldn't see her. She wondered if she had accompanied Victor to the hospital.

"Shouldn't we have mentioned our suspicions to the paramedics?" Horace said.

"I was thinking about that. You should call the hospital and alert them to the fact he might have been drugged or even poisoned. Pretend to be someone from the home. They rarely remember names nowadays and will be more interested in what you have to say than who you are."

"I'll use a staff member's name just in case. There's a public phone in the foyer, next to a noticeboard with a list of staff names and photos."

"Good. That will help get you into character. Looks like I'm going to miss breakfast. I'll speak to you when I'm released from captivity."

Marjorie hobbled inside with the aid of her cane and headed to Ruby's office, ignoring the cackle from Apollo. She was determined to keep up with her part until they had got to the bottom of whatever was going on. Doubts remained over the deaths of Edna's friends, but she was sure someone had tried to kill Victor Redman.

SEVENTEEN

Horace popped into the dining room and ate two slices of toast and marmalade swilled down by a cup of strong coffee while he waited for Marjorie to come out of Ruby's office. He watched her close the door and mouthed, "thank you" when she passed by, giving him a conspiratorial nod.

With a determined concentration, he went about his task, first scouring the noticeboard decorated with staff photographs. Beneath each photo was a name and, as Marjorie had suggested, Horace found the pictures useful for getting him into the part he was about to play. With a satisfied grin, he took a snapshot of the entire board using his mobile phone. Horace then scanned through the photos until his eyes settled on one in particular – a man he had yet to meet.

He stood around for a few more minutes, becoming more and more frustrated with people who insisted on loitering. To avoid unwanted conversations, he feigned interest in another noticeboard, his eyes scanning over the announcements and flyers posted. After what felt like an eternity, his opportunity arrived as the last client shuffled into the spacious lounge after hearing the clattering of the tea trolley. A swift glance through the slightly frosted office window revealed that Ruby Haigh was engrossed in a phone call, her headphones tightly pressed against her ears.

Horace's heart felt as if it would explode out of his chest as he frantically dialled the number for the hospital switchboard. His fingers trembled as he pressed each button. The sound of his own heartbeat filled his ears, and he was certain that anyone walking past would hear it. Finally, the call was answered, and he blurted out his urgent message, feeling breathless.

"Hello, this is Matt Friday from Evergreen Acres Retirement Homes & Rehabilitation Centre. One of our residents, a Mr Victor Redman, was admitted to your hospital a short while ago. I have some urgent information to give to the doctors treating him."

"Just one moment." Horace held his breath as he hopped from one foot to the other. The receptionist came back on the line. "He's in the Accident & Emergency department, I'll put you through now."

When someone answered, Horace launched into his rehearsed spiel, hoping he didn't sound as frantic as he felt, and praying they wouldn't ask too many probing questions. The person on the phone, who hadn't introduced herself, listened without interrupting before saying, "Hang on, I'll get the doctor treating him."

Horace's hands felt sweaty as he was put on hold again. A lightheaded feeling made him think he might pass out if he didn't get this job over with soon.

"This is Dr Shah. How can I help?"

Thankfully, Dr Shah didn't ask Horace for his name. "I'm from Evergreen Acres Retirement Homes & Rehabilitation Centre. I felt I ought to tell you that one of our carers believes the resident admitted, Mr Victor Redman, may have ingested poison or drugs."

Dr Shah sounded incredulous when asking, "Well, which was it, poison or drugs? And what precisely?"

"The carer wasn't sure about that, but she's certain he might have been given something."

"Are you implying somebody at the home has poisoned or drugged the man?"

"What's that? Sorry, doctor, I'm being called to another resident. Please could you run some tests?"

"But... Hang on a minute... What—?"

Horace slammed the receiver back in place, releasing the breath he had been holding. The hospital staff wouldn't be able to do a last-number redial because the call had gone through the main switchboard and he doubted anyone would have thought to jot down his name. Such were the impersonal ways of hospitals these days. Still, he'd done his duty.

Standing still for a few moments, he closed his eyes and took a few deep breaths to calm his racing heart and emotions. A burst of cold air from the front doors and the clattering of heels announced Edna's arrival. He opened his eyes as she came bustling in, wearing her favourite red wig, which always made him smile.

Horace felt a surge of relief.

"Hiya," she said. "Is that coffee I smell?"

He nodded weakly.

"What's the matter, Horace? You look as white as a polar bear."

Horace took a few steps towards her and kissed her on the cheek. "Let's find somewhere private and I'll tell you."

As they rounded the corner towards the smaller lounge, a screech pierced through Horace's eardrums.

"DRUGS OR POISON! POISON OR DRUGS!"

Horace grabbed Edna's arm, pulling her out of sight before anyone heard the wretched bird. As they made their way into the empty lounge, Horace caught a glimpse of Ruby's door swinging open and the woman looking around to see what the commotion was all about.

Once they were safe from prying ears, Edna couldn't hold back her cackles any longer. "I take it Apollo's outburst has got something to do with why you're looking like a bleached sink?"

Horace let out an exasperated sigh. "Will you stop with the metaphors? Blasted parrot, I forgot about him," he moaned, but soon laughed along with Edna at the absurdity of the situation. Their shared laughter brought a momentary release from the tight knot that had been building in his chest. It was a welcome distraction from the events that had transpired: finding Victor, and then making the covert phone call without being discovered. The only thing he hadn't considered was Apollo.

Once they stopped laughing, a boy, who introduced himself as Dale and told them he was on a school work placement, fetched them hot drinks. With a coffee in Edna's hand and a herbal tea in his own, Horace explained all that had happened before her visit, keeping a close eye out for anybody who might overhear the conversation.

Edna didn't seem as pleased as he'd expected her to.

"What's the matter, Edna? If Marjorie's right about what happened to Victor, it means you were right about your friends, too. You were on to something from the beginning. There is a murderer on the loose."

Edna's forehead creased in a deep frown. "I'd begun to think it was all in my head, but after Fred's discovery last night, something like this was bound to happen."

"What did Fred find?"

"The GP who certified the deaths and her husband are co-owners of this place. And, there's a tonne of money in their bank account."

"The doctor and her husband's?"

"No, the business's. Your mate Craig Tavistock could be involved in a cover-up if there is one."

Horace shook his head vigorously. "No. He wouldn't be involved in anything dodgy, and just because the doctor is co-owner doesn't mean she did anything unprofessional. She might well have believed the deaths to be natural."

"Fred's going to do a bit more digging into Dr Stephanie Branson. Her practice is about three miles from here."

"I doubt he'll find anything. I'm certain that most busy GPs would have come to the same conclusion as she did, in view of the patients' ages."

"Yeah, I guess so. What's Marge's theory again?"

Horace sighed. He worried about Edna and her inability to retain facts, but the consultant who had treated her pneumonia had told them Edna needed a long period of rehab before she would feel well again. The lack of oxygen from the scarred lung could make it difficult for her to concentrate.

"Marjorie believes Victor was poisoned or drugged, and that someone tried to make it look as if he'd choked on meat. He's not allowed solids because the Parkinson's has affected his ability to swallow, creating a choking risk."

"What makes her so sure that he didn't choke? Maybe he decided it was worth the risk to taste a bit of meat. I'm sure I would if I were in his position."

"No, you wouldn't, and Marjorie doesn't believe Victor would have put himself at risk like that. Also, his back door was unlocked. According to Marjorie, somebody poisoned or sedated him in his front room, then dragged him into the hall and stuffed meat down his throat, leaving him for dead."

"And then escaped out of the back door," said Edna. "But what if he always left his back door open? This place is safe, and it's off the beaten track."

"Off the beaten track it might be, but safe it certainly isn't with two people dead and another who might be soon. Besides, Victor wouldn't have left the back door unlocked while securing a chain at the front. It makes no sense."

"Good point. So, who wants Victor dead, and why?"

"The why's easy. As you know, Darren saw him snooping in the dead residents' apartments and everyone heard the argument, so the killer must have assumed he was getting too close. It's the who we still need to find."

"It must be Darren. If he was as upset as Marge and Isabelle said he was last night, and the two men had history, maybe he was angry enough to kill the man who hounded him for years."

"Yes, but I doubt Victor would have let him in his apartment after what had happened, especially as he suspected him of murder, and there were no signs of a break in. If Marjorie's right and Victor was moved, unless Darren's wheelchair's a phoney, he wouldn't have been capable of dragging him into the hall. We can almost rule him out."

"He could have pretended to be going to apologise and taken some sort of peace offering, and with the way he exaggerates about everything, I wouldn't put it past him to use a wheelchair he doesn't need just for the attention. His entire existence is about attention seeking."

"I suppose he could have drugged Victor first, or added something to the meat." Horace wiped his brow.

"And even if the wheelchair's for real, we can't be certain anyone moved him. Marge is not always right, you know. We need to keep an open mind."

"I hope the doctor at the hospital took me seriously and ran tests. He sounded pretty sceptical. Perhaps I should phone again and tell him what we suspect and why."

"I don't think you'll need to," said Edna.

Horace followed her gaze to the view through the window, where a police car was on its way to the entrance.

EIGHTEEN

The tests had gone well. Marjorie was told the results of her scan would be available within a day or two as it was sent straight to a specialist electronically. She might have osteoporosis considering her age, the radiographer said, but as she hadn't any symptoms, she was doing exceptionally well and wouldn't need any major intervention. Marjorie was also told by the nurse taking a batch of blood samples she wouldn't get the results until the next day.

Things went even better once she was sent to the gymnasium for her first exercise session. This was mainly because Hannah was running late and hadn't come into work yet. The physio's assistant was far more understanding about Marjorie's aversion to the equipment than Hannah would have been, and was sympathetic when he heard about the awful shock she'd had on finding the unconscious Victor Redman on the floor of his apartment.

Marjorie still hadn't eaten by the time her exercise session ended, but she was pleased to get off so lightly, although she suspected Hannah McMighty had made her intentions clear before the charade put on for Pete's sake: she would be passed over to the assistants. Well, that worked for Marjorie. Her only disappointment was to discover she had missed the tea trolley.

She looked around, hoping to glimpse someone who might get her a pot of tea. That's when she spotted a detective and a uniformed police officer in the waiting area. Marjorie presumed the woman was a detective from Ruby's body language, and this was confirmed when the officer asked her something and she sent him on his way. Horace's tip-off had at least got the police involved. Marjorie couldn't imagine they would be here about anything else.

Marjorie spied Frederick coming through the entrance, a concerned look on his face.

"Good morning," she said.

"Hello. They told me you were having physio, so I waited in the foyer for a while, and then went for a walk. Apollo kept yelling about poison and drugs. The police have not long arrived. What's going on?"

Marjorie looked over at Apollo, and he looked back. She then spotted the public phone's location. The parrot must have heard Horace's telephone conversation.

Marjorie lowered her voice. "Not here. I swear that bird knows what's going on. Have you seen Horace?"

"Yes. He and Edna are in a quiet sitting room, but as I'm not supposed to know them, I haven't spoken to them. Edna left the house earlier than me."

"Okay, let's go."

Edna smirked when Marjorie and Frederick headed their way, but said nothing else, as Marjorie could see Darren Butler moping in a corner.

"Hello again," said Horace. "How were your tests?"

"All good, thank you. I had a short exercise session in the gymnasium afterwards, which went better than expected. Hannah was delayed, and I met a charming young man who is a physio assistant. This is my friend, Frederick."

Horace feigned a polite greeting, introducing himself and Edna.

"We appear to have missed tea, and I'm parched," said Marjorie.

"Someone's just gone to fetch us a fresh pot of coffee. We can ask him to get you some tea when he comes back. Why don't you join us?"

Marjorie and Frederick sat down. She inclined her head towards Darren, and Horace nodded, whispering. "He's been sitting in that corner for half an hour. Isabelle gave him a piece of her mind."

"I see," said Marjorie.

A young man Marjorie didn't recognise brought a pot of coffee over and placed it on the table.

"This is Dale," said Horace. "He's on a school work placement."

Marjorie smiled at the boy. "Are you enjoying it?"

He nodded shyly. "It's cool. Can I get you some coffee?"

"A pot of tea for two and a few biscuits would be much appreciated," Marjorie answered.

Dale scooted away, giving Edna a red-faced look before doing so.

"Edna's been teasing the poor boy," said Horace.

"I had to pass the time somehow with him over there," Edna hissed.

Darren glared over at them. "I know you're talking about me, but it wasn't my fault what happened to Victor."

"I'm sure it wasn't," said Marjorie. "Do you know what did happen to him?"

Darren wheeled himself over to where they were sitting. "Isabelle said he choked on some meat, but I heard that copper over there mention someone from the home calling the hospital to say he was poisoned or something. Who would do that?"

"I can't imagine," said Marjorie. "Do you have any idea who might want to poison him?"

"No. I doubt anyone poisoned him at all, but if he was, it certainly wasn't by me. Okay, I was annoyed he was poking around in people's apartments. It doesn't make me a killer."

"Victor told us over dinner last night your paths had crossed before," said Marjorie.

Darren's face changed colour, and she feared he might burst a blood vessel. The veins in his neck protruded and pulsated.

"That's private business, and he had no right telling people about it."

"Perhaps we should hear your side of the story," said Horace.

"My side of the story is that it never happened the way he said it did, except in his imagination. He had no evidence and it never made it to court. The man was obsessive then and he's obsessive now, going around making everybody feel like they've got something to hide. It's not right."

"Most of us have something to hide," said Edna.

"That's as may be, but not something criminal. He has a perverse view of the world. Even his friend Isabelle knows that, and his former colleagues hated him."

"What makes you say that?" Frederick asked.

"He spoke to them like dirt. Especially the women. The man's a misogynist. I don't know what Isabelle sees in him. She and Jackie were all over him, but he's no angel."

"Jackie Bagshaw?" Edna asked. "I never noticed her speaking to him, and she was my friend."

"They had bridge nights in the bar every Monday. Maybe you weren't invited."

Edna pouted, as well she might. Marjorie wished Edna was a little less self-obsessed, as then she might have been able to tell them more about the dead man and woman, other than they played instruments and entertained people. If Victor was friends with Jackie, it explained why he might have been in her apartment. He suspected someone had killed her, as Edna did.

"You said yesterday that Victor had been in Jackie's apartment and that of another person—"

"Carl."

"Yes, Carl. Do you know what he was looking for?"

"Like I said, the man's obsessed. Most people ignore me because they think I don't listen, but I hear things. Victor thought somebody had killed them, and he didn't keep it a secret that he suspected me."

Horace feigned shock. "Really? Why would he even think that the deaths were suspicious in the first place?"

"He and Jackie talked about the possibility of somebody wanting to harm Carl after he died. Victor was always sowing bad karma. Jackie was frightened she'd be next."

"And she was," snapped Edna.

"She died next, but that don't mean anyone killed her," said Darren. "Why are you so interested, anyway?"

Marjorie was ready for the question. "Because we had the misfortune of finding Victor this morning. Isabelle was worried when he didn't appear for breakfast and Horace here had to force the door open."

"Why would you need to do that? Isabelle's got a key."

"Yes, but the safety chain was fastened."

"Victor didn't use the safety chain. I heard him tell Jackie not to use hers, either. He said if the doctor or ambulance crew ever needed to get inside, they'd wreck the door if it was fastened."

Marjorie recalled the pieces of wood on the floor after Horace burst through the door.

Horace rubbed his right shoulder. "I can assure you the chain was fastened. I'm surprised I didn't dislocate my shoulder."

Edna smirked. "It would take more than that to do you an

injury." Then she glared at Darren. "And I'm interested because Carl and Jackie were friends of mine."

"You were only here for two minutes. Why should you care?"

Marjorie was pleased Edna didn't get to reply, or Darren might have been revealing in his next story or therapy session how he'd suffered the worst emotional scarring possible from the mouth of a woman with bright red hair and a temper to match.

"Darren! Time for your aqua therapy."

Their heads spun around, relief on every face apart from Edna's at seeing Diana and Pete. Marjorie wondered how long they had been standing in the doorway and how much they might have heard. Pete didn't look happy.

After Darren left, Dale brought a pot of tea, two cups and saucers, and a plateful of luxury biscuits.

Horace took a biscuit, grinning as Dale walked away. "I saw him hovering. He probably avoids Darren, doesn't want to hear a shopping list of ailments, poor kid."

"That man nearly got a piece of my mind."

"Your temper, more like," Frederick muttered, but was ignored.

"Pete looked proper cheesed off," said Edna.

"I expect his idea of Evergreen Acres being a utopia for the elderly is being chipped away," said Frederick.

"Decimated more like," Edna chortled, and Horace sniggered.

Frederick rolled his eyes, saying, "I haven't had the chance to ask, but I take it from what Darren was saying just now that something happened to Victor this morning?"

Horace filled Frederick in on the early morning events while Marjorie poured the tea. She took a few biscuits from the plate, which Horace had moved to the centre of the table before Edna scoffed the lot.

"Has anyone heard how Victor is?" Marjorie asked.

Horace shook his head. "I've been keeping away from that bird who's been spouting about my conversation over and over. He heard the telephone call and I'm sure he'll give me away if I go anywhere near his cage. I'm also avoiding the plods, to be honest."

"Not anymore," said Frederick, grinning.

"I'm looking for Mr Horace Tyler and Lady Marjorie Snellthorpe," the detective announced, entering the room.

"You've found them," said Edna. "This is Horace, and that's Marge."

Marjorie scowled at Edna for the slip up over her name, but Edna was oblivious.

The detective's eyes crinkled momentarily. "I'm Detective Sergeant Moira Frame. Do you mind if I ask you a few questions?"

"Of course not, DS Frame. Tea?" Marjorie offered.

"If there's coffee in that pot, I don't mind if I do." DS Frame took a seat.

NINETEEN

It didn't take long for Marjorie to work out why DS Frame hadn't separated them for questioning. After Horace persuaded Dale to bring a fresh pot of coffee and a mug, the DS closed the doors behind the boy.

"I'm commandeering this room," she told her colleague. "Make sure no-one comes in."

"Right, Sarge," the officer replied, taking up guard duty.

"I would normally question you individually, but your reputation as amateur sleuths precedes you."

"Golly," said Marjorie. "How can that be?"

"Mrs Parkinton was on the local news a few months ago and her sleuthing came up." The detective smiled at Edna. "I loved your story about the enormous selection of wigs and how you deal with hair loss after undergoing chemotherapy. It was inspirational. I recognise that one from the interview."

Edna patted her favourite red wig, proudly. "Really? I don't see myself as inspirational, but if you—"

"Who else would have seen that interview?" Marjorie glared at Edna.

"Don't worry, Marge, they aired it at 3am. I can't imagine

anyone who lives here having watched it. Nobody mentioned it when I was staying."

"Nevertheless, I'd thank you to avoid wearing the red wig from today."

"Point taken," said Edna, but she grinned at the friendly detective. "We're famous, then?"

DS Frame took a slurp of coffee, her eyes turning more serious. "As much as I enjoyed your story, we don't like amateurs interfering with police matters. When I was given the names of the two people who found Mr Redman this morning, yours stood out, Lady Snellthorpe."

"Call me Marjorie, please."

Edna switched in a flash from preening to affronted, harrumphing. "Why hers?"

Horace patted Edna's arm. "It's the title, Edna. And you weren't with us this morning when we found poor Victor, or DS Frame would have recognised yours."

"You, I assume, are Frederick Mackworth?" DS Frame eyed the former pharmacist.

"Yes, Sergeant."

"In which case, I'd like to know what the four of you are doing here?" DS Frame remained friendly, but she was nobody's fool.

"Marjorie had a fall," said Horace.

"And lost confidence," added Frederick.

"And I had a cataract operation."

"The administrator, Ms Haigh, has informed me that Mr Horace Tyler and Lady Marjorie Snellthorpe only met yesterday, so unless you would like me to enlighten her and charge you with wasting police time, I suggest you tell me the truth."

Edna pouted again. "That is the truth, apart from them not knowing each other."

DS Frame's eyes hardened and Marjorie felt it preferable to

keep her on side. "The sergeant will not fall for our story, Edna. I suggest we tell her everything."

Edna sighed heavily. "You're gonna think it's mad."

"Let me be the judge of that," said DS Frame, refilling her mug and sitting back. "Humour me."

With each of them interjecting at different points, Edna told the detective about her genuine rehab stay and about her suspicions after two of her seemingly healthy friends died suddenly. When they reached the point of the undercover work, DS Frame couldn't hide a smirk, especially when Frederick told her about Marjorie's introduction to the gymnasium. The detective's eyes appraised each of them as they spoke, and Marjorie could understand why she might think they had taken things too far with their dubious fake cover stories.

"We weren't sure whether there was anything to Edna's fears at first, but as she was so upset about the loss of her two friends, we couldn't do nothing," said Marjorie.

"Why didn't you raise your concerns with the police?" DS Frame asked Edna.

"Because you would have thought I was a neurotic old woman with a conspiracy theory."

"Perhaps, but not necessarily," said DS Frame looking thoughtful.

"And there's no proof that anything is, or was, amiss, and a doctor certified their deaths as resulting from natural causes," explained Horace. "You said it yourself, Sergeant. We didn't want to waste police time."

"I understand. But you're happy to waste your own time."

"And money," said Frederick. "This place costs a fortune."

"We have plenty of both," said Horace. "If Edna's suspicions turned out to be unfounded, no-one would have been the wiser and we would have had a pleasant stay in a rather plush establishment."

"But now you believe there's something to Edna's story

because of what happened to Mr Redman. I assume you know he's a former detective inspector?"

"We do," said Marjorie.

"And I take it one of you called the hospital mentioning poison and drugs? The administrator believes someone used the public telephone to call, and that wouldn't have been a member of staff. She thought it might have been Mrs Stoppard, but the hospital doctor said it was a man he spoke to."

"Guilty as charged," said Horace, lowering his eyes. "Marjorie suspected Victor was poisoned or drugged before someone forced the meat into his throat to try to make it look like a choking accident, and we didn't want Victor to die because of our neglecting to mention it."

"Mr Redman certainly wasn't poisoned," DS Frame said emphatically.

"Oh dear. We really have wasted your time," said Marjorie.

"Not quite. He wasn't poisoned with any substance, from tests the hospital has run so far, but neither did he choke. He had large amounts of sleeping pills in his system, suggesting he may have taken an overdose. If it weren't for the presence of the meat, I would look at attempted suicide, but there is significant bruising around the oropharynx, suggesting it could have happened as you suspect."

"Do you believe that's what happened?" Marjorie asked.

"As we say in the force, we're keeping an open mind. It may well be an attempted suicide where he himself forced the meat down after taking the pills to make sure he didn't bring them back up."

"Or we're right and someone around here wants him dead," snapped Edna.

DS Frame didn't seem offended by Edna's tone. In fact, she appeared amused by it.

"What we have found out from the residents and staff we have spoken to so far is that Mr Redman has always refused to use the security chain inside his flat. He told Mrs Stoppard that during his time in the police force, he broke his shoulder after forcing open a door with a chain, and if it hadn't been there, he might have saved a woman's life. That, and the fact he didn't want to put anyone else through the pain that followed, was the reason he gave for not using the chain."

"I can vouch for the pain," said Horace, rubbing his right shoulder. "I'm just grateful it wasn't a composite door."

"Darren Butler told us Victor discouraged Jackie Bagshaw from using the chain because help might not arrive quickly enough if she was taken ill and they had to break down the door," Marjorie added.

DS Frame nodded. "Nevertheless, this knowledge could support the theory of attempted suicide and that, on this occasion, he deliberately used the chain to reduce the likelihood of help getting to him in time."

"But then why leave the back door open?" Marjorie quizzed.

"Indeed," said DS Frame. "Did any of you witness the argument between Mr Butler and Mr Redman yesterday evening?"

"I did," said Marjorie. "Darren accused Victor of snooping inside the dead residents' apartments. I think you should know Darren Butler and Victor had history."

"Yes, Mrs Stoppard mentioned that. He was arrested but never charged over the death of his mother-in-law. Did Mr Butler mention it?"

"I told him Victor had shared how their paths had crossed in the past. He denies doing anything wrong back then and insists Victor was obsessional and hated to be wrong. Isabelle implied the same thing to me, except she likes Victor. Victor admitted to me and Isabelle last night there wasn't enough proof to take the case to trial. But he remained convinced Darren killed his mother-in-law for money."

"Hmm." DS Frame seemed thoughtful.

"Darren also told us Victor was unpopular with his colleagues. Did you know him?"

"Long before my time, I'm afraid, but I'll see what I can find out. I think that's all the questions I have for now. I have a forensic team going through Mr Redman's apartment. We're treating this incident at the moment as suspicious, but you must prepare yourself for an attempted suicide outcome. I understand Mr Redman was already an unhappy man and Mrs Stoppard believes the argument yesterday may have tipped him over the edge."

"What about my friends, Jackie and Carl?" Edna asked.

"All I can promise is that I'll talk to the doctor who certified the deaths and if I'm not satisfied with what he says, I'll speak to my DI."

"The doctor's a she," said Frederick. "And she's co-owner of all this." He moved his eyes to convey it was the home he was referring to.

"That's interesting, but not surprising, and not necessarily suspicious. A lot of GPs invest in care facilities, it doesn't mean they are dishonest. Your friends may have died from preexisting medical conditions, otherwise the GP would have requested post-mortems. If you want my advice, I'd pack up and go home now, and leave matters to the police."

Edna huffed.

"We'd like to stay a little longer. We've paid for four nights and we're enjoying ourselves," said Horace.

DS Frame fixed her eyes on Marjorie. "As long as you and your friends realise this isn't a game. I won't mention your little charade to anyone for now, but if you get in my way, I won't hesitate to send you packing myself."

"We won't get in your way, Sergeant Frame," said Marjorie.

"And you must be careful, because if by some stretch of the imagination you're right and there is a killer in this home, I don't want the body count going up any further." The sergeant was frowning, as though already regretting her decision.

"Will Victor recover?" Marjorie asked.

"It's unlikely. The consultant I spoke to says he was outliving his prognosis anyway, but they will do everything they can. I'm afraid they won't attempt to resuscitate him if he goes into cardiac arrest. If, by some miracle, he wakes up, they will let me know straightaway. Now I'd better get on. Please call the station if you have anything else to tell me, and I mean it when I say it, don't do anything silly."

"Thank you, Sergeant Frame, for not treating us like senile busybodies," Marjorie said.

DS Frame chuckled. "The jury's out on that one."

"I like her," said Horace as soon as she left.

"I do too," said Frederick, "but I wonder if she's right about packing it in and letting the police get on with the investigation."

"Pah. That's not going to happen," said Edna, glowering at him.

"I don't know about you three, but I'm ravenous," said Marjorie. "I believe that's the lunch gong."

TWENTY

After finishing lunch, Edna and Horace took a leisurely stroll through the expansive gardens, eager to strike up conversations with anyone who might have known Carl and Jackie to see if they had any opinions about their recent deaths. Edna asked Horace to show her Victor's apartment, although he didn't need to, as the striped police cordon was a dead giveaway.

Edna would have liked to go inside, but the cordon blocked their path. Horace was cautious. Even though there was no sign of activity, he didn't want to risk entering during daylight hours when they might be caught.

"Best leave any rummaging until after dark. I can go with Marjorie if we need to."

"Fine." Edna was feeling glum, despite being an inspiration to DS Frame. She couldn't shake off a melancholic sense of exclusion. Knowing that her friends were simply following her lead didn't lessen the feeling, and the emotions still weighed heavily.

They had been walking for nearly an hour without seeing a single person. It appeared the inhabitants of the apartments had gone into hibernation and the other residents were most likely in the gym.

"Have you had any of those pretend eye drops yet?" Edna asked.

"Diana instilled them when you popped to the loo this morning. I'll get some more later. The staff have been distracted."

"You're telling me!" Edna spotted Timmy stalking the grounds, searching for prey, but Jackie had attached a bell to his collar to give wildlife a fair warning that he was around. Instead, he chased leaves. "Jackie loved that cat, you know."

"I can see why. He's a beauty." Giving up on catching anything useful, Timmy paused for a fuss. Horace bent down to stroke him. "He's a handsome fellow, I'll give him that. I love his pink nose."

Seeing the beloved cat of her late friend only added to Edna's gloom. "It's getting chilly out here," she said with a shiver. "Perhaps we should try to speak with that Isabelle woman. Do you know which apartment is hers?"

Horace straightened up, rubbing his back. Timmy, annoyed his pampering had been interrupted, let out a low growl before scampering off into the bushes.

"That's a good idea, Edna. I think I know which one it is, and there's no time like the present." Horace set off at a brisk pace that caught Edna by surprise. Her body protested as she struggled to keep up. The pneumonia had robbed her of her strength and her breath, and every step felt like an uphill battle. During her days at the care home, this wouldn't have been an issue since no-one rushed anywhere, except for Diana Ferrett, who was always in a hurry. But now, watching her friends gallivanting around like they were still young and spry made Edna feel old and tired. It wasn't a feeling she enjoyed or wanted to admit to.

"I tell you what," she called after Horace. "You see Isabelle, and I'll try to catch a word with Diana. She's always got something to say. Plus, it would be nice if I can see Eleanor. She's quiet, but listens. Whether she'll remember what she's heard is another matter, but I haven't seen her since we admitted you."

Horace paused to let Edna catch up. "I don't remember you mentioning an Eleanor."

"Then you weren't listening. I told you about her last night. She was the fourth person in our musical quartet. She's a wealthy widow and plays the piano beautifully. I bet she's upset about Jackie; they were close. I'll see if she wants to come to the funeral tomorrow."

"What's she like?"

'Gorgeous for her age' was what Edna could have said, but she had a feeling Horace and Eleanor would hit it off better than she would like them to. She hated herself for feeling envious, but she couldn't bear to lose Horace's friendship, especially when she thought she might be approaching her last act.

"Eleanor's quiet and shy, which is why I need to talk to her alone."

Horace raised a quizzical eyebrow, but shrugged his shoulders. "Okay. Shall we meet for afternoon tea?"

"Yep, or dinner. We should be able to have a catchup with Marge and Fred by then without it looking like we know each other well."

Edna took a few minutes to catch her breath after Horace's departure. The autumn sun cast a dappled glow through the trees, and a gentle breeze rustled the leaves. She closed her eyes and breathed slowly like the medical staff had taught her. In, out, in, out, allowing the crisp air to replenish her energy.

A few deep inhales and exhales did the trick. Her enthusiasm for what they were doing returned, and she was ready for the chase. With slow, purposeful steps, she made her way back inside, shedding her coat by the door before continuing with renewed vigour.

"PAIN IN STOMACH. BAD PAIN. WORST PAIN."

Edna chortled, giving Apollo a thumbs up. "Thanks for the warning," she said. Darren must be somewhere in the vicinity, so she checked around her. She'd leave him to Marge and Fred. Edna had no reserves of patience left in her to listen to any more of his moaning.

Edna's face lit up when she saw Diana's wide smile.

"Hello, Edna. Where's your friend?"

"He wanted a longer walk now he can see again. I thought I'd come inside and have a chat with Eleanor. Any idea where she is?"

"She was in the library about ten minutes ago." Diana's expression clouded. "I haven't had the heart to tell her about Victor yet. She's been so cut up about Jackie's death."

"That's understandable. I feel the same. I won't mention Victor. Any news on that front?"

Diana shook her head. "Pete doesn't think he'll survive. Did you know the police have been here asking questions?"

"Yes, the sergeant spoke to Horace, and the woman called Marjorie. They found him this morning. Horace said it was just routine."

"Humph. Somebody's been mischief-making, according to Pete."

"Really? How?"

Diana glanced around before lowering her voice. "Someone called the hospital from the public phone to say Victor had been drugged or poisoned. Can you believe that?"

"There are some strange people in this place," said Edna.

"It was a man, and between you and me, it wouldn't surprise me if it was Darren."

"But didn't he have an argument with Victor yesterday? That would make him look like the prime suspect."

"Exactly. But as Victor wasn't poisoned, it makes him my prime suspect as a troublemaker. They're saying Victor took matters into his own hands with an overdose of sleeping tablets."

"That's sad."

"I know. Obviously, Darren didn't help things with all his shouting yesterday. I expect you heard about that. He took us all by surprise with that outburst. I didn't know he had it in him."

"Me neither," said Edna. "It's a shame I missed it, but on the other hand, it's as well I did."

Diana winked. "I know what you mean." She then motioned with her head to the large parrot cage. "Apollo knows who made that call, but he's not saying."

Edna cackled. "I shouldn't laugh because nobody should waste police time."

"And no-one should create trouble for Pete. He's got enough on his plate as it is, trying to keep *her* under control."

Edna's eyebrows rose in amazement as Marjorie's intuition had once again been proved correct. Diana did have eyes for Pete. It was clear from the way she spoke about him.

Edna turned to see who Diana meant by *her* and watched Hannah McManus hanging up her coat.

"Why? What's she done?"

"I probably shouldn't gossip, but since you're no longer staying with us, it won't do any harm." Diana shot her a sly smile. "Pete doesn't say much about it, but I know he believes Hannah is out of control. She comes and goes as she pleases and hardly seems to do any work. Just look at today, for example. It's well past lunchtime and she should have been here first thing this morning, and yet here she is, strolling in like she owns the place, acting like the Queen of blessed Sheba. Next, she'll start dishing out her orders like she's the boss or something."

As if to prove the point, Hannah marched up to the two women. Ignoring Edna as though she were invisible, she barked at Diana.

"Get Mr Washington down for his assessment in ten minutes. I've got a few things to do first."

Open-mouthed, both women stared after Hannah, who marched through a door into the corridor reserved for staff only.

"Blimey, I see what you mean," said Edna. "That Lady Marjorie Snellthorpe hasn't taken to her either. She told me and Horace over dinner last night."

"One day, Hannah will go too far."

Edna was shocked at the ferocity of tone and the dark hatred in Diana's eyes.

"It's been nice to chat," she said hastily. "I'd better see if I can find Eleanor before Horace comes back from his walk."

"And I'd better help Pete with the care plans... after I've passed on the message to Mr Washington, of course."

Diana was smiling again. Edna would hate to see the young woman's enthusiasm for her job quashed by someone like Hannah McManus. It would be so unfair.

TWENTY-ONE

When Isabelle opened the door to her apartment, Horace could hear the faint murmur of voices in the background.

"Hello, Horace." Isabelle greeted him with a warm smile as she opened the door wider. Despite the shock of the morning, she had taken time to apply makeup and was stoical. "I'm pleased to see you. I haven't had a chance to thank you properly for what you did earlier."

"Think nothing of it. I hope I'm not disturbing you, but I just wanted to check on you after the traumatic events. You and Victor seem close."

"How perceptive of you. Few men care about such things, but you're not disturbing me. Please come inside. Marjorie and her friend Frederick are here on a similar mission. I was just about to make tea, would you like some?"

"If it's not too much of an imposition."

"It isn't."

Horace followed her into the apartment, taking in the elegant decor and cosy atmosphere. The walls were adorned with still-life paintings and photographs of Isabelle with various celebrities, he assumed, she had interviewed over the years. Everything was stylish and easy on the eye.

It was clear that Isabelle had a talent for design and a love of eclectic art. Unlike Victor's apartment, hers had a homely feel. Its charming atmosphere was no doubt a reflection of its glamorous owner. Victor's apartment had felt more like student digs than a home.

Isabelle led him into a sitting room at the rear. Large windows let in plenty of natural light, giving it a warm and inviting feel. Horace settled into one of the comfortable armchairs as Isabelle prepared tea.

"Hello again." Horace nodded to Marjorie and extended a hand towards Fred. "I wanted to check Isabelle had recovered from her ordeal this morning. It appears we had the same idea."

"Indeed," said Marjorie. "We've not long arrived."

"Well, it's kind of you all to enquire after my health because I must admit, it was quite a shock finding Victor like that. If it weren't for Horace and you, Marjorie, I'm not sure he would be alive. As it is..." Her voice trailed off.

"Let me help you with that." Horace took the tea tray from Isabelle's shaking hands before it landed on the floor. He placed it down on a square coffee table, noticing more quality. Isabelle recovered and fetched a plate of biscuits from the kitchen while Horace placed coasters around the table for the fine china cups and saucers. Marjorie would be feeling in her element.

With teacups and saucers in everyone's hands, Horace asked if Isabelle had heard anything from the hospital. Isabelle's hand trembled again as she set her teacup back on to its delicate saucer and placed them both on the table.

"I received a phone call about an hour ago." Blinking a few times to ward away the tears threatening to fall, she added, "Seemingly, they believe the silly man took an overdose. I can tell you now, they're wrong about that."

"How can you be so sure?" Horace asked.

"Victor's a Catholic. Maybe not a practising one, but he would view suicide as a mortal sin. He's said as much when talking about people he dealt with who had taken their own lives. No heaven for them, he'd say."

"Although I believe the Catholic Church has become more forgiving in recent times," said Fred.

"But Victor's view on the matter hadn't changed. He'd have told me if it had," said Isabelle.

"But if he was desperate," argued Fred.

Isabelle shook her head. "No. When Victor left the dining room last night, he was on a mission to put Darren Butler away once and for all. I could see it in his eyes. He wouldn't have taken an overdose."

"I have to say, I agree with Isabelle. Victor was upset, but more determined than distraught when he left the table," said Marjorie. "Of course, no-one can know what his mood was later."

"The doctor also informed me that the stubborn man's put me, rather than his daughter, down as his next of kin."

"I take it you weren't aware of that?" Marjorie said gently.

Isabelle shook her head, a mixture of hurt and understanding in her eyes. "He never asked me, but I suppose I shouldn't be surprised. He and his daughter haven't spoken for decades."

"Is there a wife?" Fred asked, brows furrowed.

"They divorced when his daughter, Siobhan, was five. I think his wife died a few years back, I don't remember. His divorce was a difficult topic and one he preferred not to dwell on. He would have felt a failure."

"Does he believe divorce is a sin as well?" Fred asked.

"I suppose he may do. Victor rarely shares personal details with anyone. He will gladly talk for hours about the cases he has worked on or the arrests he made, but he always changes the subject if it becomes too personal. I suppose that's why he didn't tell me he'd made me his next of kin."

Horace noticed Marjorie fixing her gaze on Isabelle, as if preparing for something.

"I hope this doesn't sound impertinent, but after my recent fall, I carried out some research into the cost of leasing apartments here. There's a long waiting list, which doesn't surprise me. But I couldn't help wondering how a retired detective like Victor can afford a place such as this."

"I don't consider it impertinent, Marjorie, but Victor would. I tried to broach the subject with him once, but he became so angry that I knew better than to bring the topic up again. As I said before, he's a private man when it comes to personal matters."

"Maybe he made some wise investments in his early days," Fred suggested.

Isabelle shook her head. "I doubt it. From what little details he shared about his ex-wife, theirs was an acrimonious divorce where, in his words, 'she fleeced him', so I don't think he would have been able to save until much later in life."

"He'd get a good pension, I suppose," said Marjorie.

"Not enough for a place like this," said Horace. "He could have inherited the money."

"That's what I assumed," said Isabelle, "because I didn't, and don't, want to consider any other options." Isabelle's words hung in the air, heavy with unspoken implications.

Such as police corruption, thought Horace. He cleared his throat, trying to push away those thoughts.

"Did the hospital give any indication of a potential recovery? The police sergeant we spoke to wasn't optimistic."

"Neither was the doctor who spoke to me on the telephone. He told me to prepare myself. I don't know whether to phone his daughter."

"I would have thought she should know," said Fred.

"Me too, but Victor would be so angry with me for interfering."

"But surely if he named you as his next of kin, then he left that kind of decision to you," said Marjorie.

Isabelle dabbed her eyes, looking more confident. "You're right. I'll call her as soon as you've gone, or get Ruby to. They must have her telephone number here, because I don't."

"That's settled, then," said Marjorie.

Isabelle picked her tea up again, looking around at them. "It was odd about the police being called, wasn't it?"

"I assumed they came as a matter of routine." Marjorie's eyes were unblinking and unreadable. She was so much better at this sort of thing than Horace was.

Isabelle spoke again. "Diana believes it was Darren stirring up trouble. She says a man phoned the hospital and suggested someone had drugged or poisoned Victor. I hope he hasn't opened a hornet's nest."

"Because of their shared past, or because of what we were discussing about Victor's funds?" Marjorie asked.

"Both, I suppose. Darren was angry enough to do something ridiculous yesterday, but whether the animosity carried over to this morning, I don't know," said Isabelle. "I challenged him on the matter. I even accused him of being the one to supply Victor with the meat he choked on."

"He told us," said Horace.

Isabelle appeared surprised.

"Darren was moping around when we were having coffee this morning, then he had a go at us, accusing us of thinking the same thing."

"Do you think Darren is capable of doing either?" Marjorie asked.

"If you'd asked me that question before yesterday, I would have said no, but after seeing how he behaved yesterday afternoon, I wouldn't be so certain. Plus, I didn't know then that

Victor had accused him of murder in the past. Who knows? He might have gone to see Victor last night and taken something with him, but I don't think Victor would have let him in. As for the telephone call to the hospital, I believe he could have done that."

"But why?" Fred asked. "Surely he'd be incriminating himself."

"Unless he was using reverse psychology," offered Marjorie.

Isabelle appeared confused. "What do you mean?"

"It's like the murderer who hangs about at a crime scene, pretending to be an innocent bystander, but all the while challenging the police to catch him, or her."

"How perverse," said Isabelle. "But you could be right. I think Darren is trying to deflect any suspicion away from himself and is hoping the police will investigate Victor and his past. They'll rake everything up and look into whether there were any shady dealings in relation to how he gained his money. If there were... Well..."

"You mean Darren wants his revenge on Victor for accusing him of murder?" said Horace.

"Something like that. But if he made that telephone call, he's a cruel and heartless man. As if Victor hasn't suffered enough." This time, the tears fell.

Horace was pleased no-one was looking at him, because the heat in his face would have been a dead giveaway.

TWENTY-TWO

Not being a lover of books, Edna hadn't been inside the library during her rehab stay. In fact, she couldn't remember being shown it during her initial tour of the home, but she hadn't been well, so it might have to be put down as a lapse of memory.

It was a beautiful modern room, unlike Marjorie's more formal library. A domed skylight flooded it with autumnal sunlight. There were a dozen or so small tables placed within reach of cushioned seats. Three enormous bright-white contraptions like space-age pods dominated the fringes of the room. Edna couldn't resist placing a hand on one of them. It spun around, revealing a huge chasm lined with fluffy cushions. As comfortable as it might look, she was certain that if she ever sat inside, she would not get out again. And if Marjorie attempted the feat, she would be lost forever. Edna cackled at the image forming in her head.

"I'd recognise that laugh anywhere." One of the very contraptions Edna had been looking at spun around with her friend Eleanor buried inside.

"How the heck do you get out of that monstrosity?"

"It takes practice, but I've got it down to a fine art now.

Watch." Eleanor leaned forward, placing the book she was reading to one side. She then shuffled until she could reach the sides of the domed opening. With a few grunts and a lot more shuffling, she managed to move herself into a position where her feet dangled a few inches above the floor. One more heave, and Eleanor landed. "See. It's not that difficult."

"If you say so." It had looked incredibly difficult from where Edna was standing.

"Pete told me a friend of yours was in for rehab. I was hoping you might say hello and here you are." There was a dullness in Eleanor's eyes as she and Edna ambled across to sit in two of the more traditional reading chairs next to a freshly polished dark oak table.

"I asked Diana, and she told me where to find you," said Edna. "I heard about Jackie on the day I was checking out. It was such a shock. How are you?"

Eleanor's eyes misted up. "I miss her. And Carl. They were my two best friends."

"It must have been a blow, Jackie dying so soon after Carl. I was quite upset about it myself."

Eleanor used a lace-edged handkerchief to dab her eyes. Edna surmised she wore expensive mascara because it didn't smear like Edna's would have done if she'd dared do that. Applying layers of makeup was one of the things she, Jackie, and Eleanor had in common. Even on her worst days, Edna would spend as long as it took in front of the mirror. Before going anywhere, she would choose what colour wig to wear, and that was always followed by applying makeup to match. The only advantage of permanent alopecia – a side effect of the chemotherapy she'd had for cancer – was that she could change her hair colour and style every day without having to go to the hairdresser's. Sometimes, she would take her wigs to a local woman for a restyle. Her own attempts at restyling had ended up with catastrophic consequences, and Horace having to buy her two new wigs.

"I mistakenly assumed Jackie would live forever. I don't suppose you've heard, but there are murmurings her death wasn't natural."

"Really? What murmurings?"

"The staff assume that because we are all getting on, we're in our dotage, but people are whispering, you know?"

"What are they suggesting?"

"Well, you know how angry Carl and Jackie were about the home not providing enough entertainment, outings, and the like. Some of the others are suggesting one of the staff did them in to shut them up."

"That's drastic, isn't it? Do they have any evidence?"

"Most of the apartment residents, including that ex-detective, believe it. Isabelle Stoppard pooh-poohs it and I must admit it sounds farfetched. It's given people something to talk about, but I find it frightening. I don't like to think there's a killer among the staff."

"I can imagine. Do these whisperers have any suspects?" Edna wanted to take advantage of Eleanor's lucid moment, not knowing when her friend might forget what they were talking about.

Eleanor looked up from her eye-dabbing, forcing a smile. "Plenty, and they range from the credible to the realms of fantasy. Someone even suggested it might be Peter Grabham."

"Never!" Edna's thoughts turned to the dedicated senior nurse for a moment. "He might take himself seriously at times, but I can't see him killing anyone. If I remember right, he agreed with their complaints on the quiet, like."

"Did he? I don't recall. Oh yes, I do, you're right, he did. I don't think I can stay here any longer, Edna. I've been looking at other homes."

"That's sad. I was hoping to visit you regularly once I got back to my normal self."

Eleanor's eyes brightened. "Were you? That would be wonderful. It might make it worth staying if I had a friend. My family live so far away."

Edna swallowed a lump in her throat. She hadn't even bothered to ask her friend about family. All she knew was that Eleanor was a wealthy widow.

"Where do they live?"

"I have a son, daughter-in-law, three grandchildren and a great grandson... There might be more I've never met. He lives somewhere in Australia. There are two married daughters in Ontario, Canada, one with kids, the other without, and my younger son is a lay preacher in Tanzania."

"Blimey! They are spread out. Where were you from originally?"

"Ontario, that's why I remember where my daughters live in Canada. They were born there and couldn't wait to go back. We moved over here in the sixties, which is why I've lost my accent."

Not entirely. Edna had detected one and assumed Eleanor was American, but she wasn't good at differentiating between the US and Canadian accents. She could identify most English accents down to cities or counties, but that was about her limit. Marjorie would know straight away where Eleanor came from.

"Do you ever think of moving closer to them?"

Eleanor shook her head. "That would mean having to choose which one to burden, and I could never do that. I love them all, and I'm proud of what they've achieved in life, but I don't want any of them to have to look after me. It's not as though I can't afford the care."

Edna had always longed to have children, but when she met people like Eleanor, it made her realise that even if she had, there was no guarantee they would be close. She was as independent as Eleanor, so it would likely make no difference to her life as it was now. There was no use dwelling on such things.

"Tell me more about these rumours."

"What rumours?"

"The rumours about our friends being murdered."

"Oh yes. There's not a lot to say. All I've heard is that Pete was on the scene at the time, or soon after each death, which I suppose is why people are latching on to him as a suspect."

"But he would be on the scene, wouldn't he? He's the senior nurse and would be called to attend. I've often seen him and Diana flying off to the next emergency. It's what they do. Besides, I can't see Pete having a motive for killing our friends. It's not as if he owns the place, is it?"

"That's true, but he's so very proud of its reputation. If there is a killer in our midst, I'd put my money on the physio. She's the nastiest person in the home, closely followed by Ruby Haigh."

Edna considered Hannah for a moment, and how Diana said she came and went as she pleased. There was no doubt in her mind that Horace and Marge should try to wheedle more details about what the maverick physiotherapist was up to. A visit to her office might be called for.

"I only met Hannah once, and I didn't like her, but that doesn't make her a killer. The only ones who would suffer from Carl and Jackie's complaints would be those in management. Has anyone spoken to the police?"

"I didn't think they had, but I noticed a police car outside today, so perhaps somebody has. This is the first time I've been out of my apartment for days. After Jackie died, I wanted to be alone."

Edna couldn't bring herself to mention the police visit being related to what had happened to Victor. Eleanor would hear about the events of this morning soon enough, but it wouldn't be from her.

"I found out Jackie's funeral is tomorrow. Are you going?"

"Oh, I'd forgotten about that. I wasn't sure if I'd feel well enough. I've arranged for a wreath and given to her favourite cat charity." Eleanor rubbed her head.

"Is that the charity that donated Timmy? I saw him when I was out for a walk just now."

"He misses Jackie terribly. I'm always having to shoo him away from her front door... I'm feeling a little better... Will you be there?"

When Eleanor was tired, she missed words and jumped sentences, and Edna wouldn't get much more sensible conversation if she didn't take the opportunity.

"Yes, I thought I'd go along. We could sit together if you like." Edna might have to tell Eleanor about Fred and what they were up to or tell him to give the funeral a miss.

"In that case, I'll be there. I'd like to pay my respects and Diana's got the day off. She offered to give me a lift."

Why hadn't Edna and Marge thought that staff or residents from the home would attend the funeral? Fred would have to bow out and she'd go alone, but at least she'd have people she knew to speak to. She was pleased Diana had thought to offer to take Eleanor.

"That's good of her. She'll make an excellent nurse one day."

"I don't know why she doesn't get on with her training now. If it's money or sponsorship she needs, I'm sure there are plenty of people here who would support her, me included."

"Maybe she doesn't have enough confidence yet, and I doubt she'd be allowed to take money from residents," said Edna.

"You could be right. Anyway, Edna, you've brightened up my day, but I mustn't keep you from your friend any longer. I'm going to head back to my apartment for dinner. I'll see you tomorrow."

TWENTY-THREE

The dinner gong sounded just as Edna turned up. Marjorie was pleased to see her friend looking animated and much more like her old self. She was even walking better and didn't appear to be gasping for breath.

"Shall we eat in the larger dining room and have a chat?" Edna suggested once she arrived. "There's more space for privacy in there and I've just seen Darren heading to the residents' dining room."

Marjorie voiced her opinion. "I expect he's happy Victor won't be in there."

"Unless he always dines there," said Horace.

"Nope. He usually targets the short-stayers with stories about his ailments. The apartment residents have heard it all before, so they avoid him," said Edna.

Marjorie was almost tempted to go through just to see who he was setting his sights on, but guessed it would be Isabelle. "Off to the large dining room it is, then," she said.

The larger dining room's tables were well spaced out with most people occupying two large, round tables next to the windows. Marjorie opted for one well away from those already settled. Once the four of them were seated with dinner ordered, she shared with Edna what they had found out from Isabelle. Which, she had to admit, wasn't much.

"One unanswered question our conversation highlighted was in relation to where Victor got the money to pay for his lease, because a retired detective's pension wouldn't cover it. Isabelle has also concluded that Darren was the one who called the hospital. She postulates his motivation is to prompt the police to investigate Victor's finances."

Edna nudged Horace. "Diana said the same thing to me. Not about the money, but about Darren looking to cause trouble."

"I must admit, I feel terrible every time the subject comes up, and it seems unfair to let people point the finger at Darren," Horace admitted. "I'd rather confess, I was never a good liar."

Edna smirked. "You managed to keep your indiscretions from your wife often enough."

"That's enough of that, Edna!" Marjorie chastised. "We know how much Horace regrets his past. None of us are without things we regret."

"Yes, as a well-known Bible quote says, 'Let him who is without sin throw the first stone,'" added Frederick.

Edna glared at him. "All right, Mr High and Mighty. Sorry, Horace." She at least had the decency to check Horace was okay.

"It's all right," he mumbled, but there was a mixture of hurt and sorrow in his eyes. Marjorie thought he was much more sensitive than he made out sometimes.

During dinner, they chatted about other things. Marjorie hoped they could maintain their cover, despite the unwelcome news that Edna had been boasting about their exploits on television. It was unlikely people in the home would remember their names anyway, and if any of them had recognised Edna, they would have said so when she was staying for her own rehab.

"Tell me more about your television appearance," Marjorie said.

"It was not about our sleuthing if that's what you mean. A friend's son who's a producer wanted me to talk about my life as a singer. He was also interested in my cancer treatment. The sleuthing only came up because I mentioned your shock at my changing hair colours when we met up after years of not seeing each other. The interviewer asked a few questions about the sleuthing, but our time was almost up by then."

Marjorie felt reassured by Edna's explanation. "Why air the programme in the middle of the night?"

"TV channels have to fill the airwaves, Marge. I can't say I enjoyed the time slot; it took hours to put a new lot of makeup on. But at least they sent a taxi to collect me and take me home."

"I taped it and watched it the next day. It didn't occur to me that anyone like the detective sergeant would watch," said Horace.

Frederick finished up the last of his meal. "Maybe she was pulling a night shift."

"Or she has a baby," said Marjorie.

Edna appeared to be losing patience and, unusually, didn't seem interested in continuing the conversation about her television interview. After wolfing down a beef stew as though she hadn't eaten in weeks, she put her cutlery down and stared wild-eyed at them.

"You haven't asked how I got on."

"With your friend? We were assuming you would tell us once we had finished eating," said Marjorie.

"Before I found Eleanor, I had quite a chat with Diana, who's not a fan of Hannah McManus, I can tell you. She reckons the woman should get the sack. Comes and goes as she likes and thinks she's the boss."

Marjorie swallowed her last mouthful of quiche and sighed.

"There are far too many people like Hannah in the world, but it isn't a crime."

"Except she's robbing her employer if she isn't pulling her weight," said Frederick. "I only had to sack one man in all my years of running a pharmacy, and it was for that very reason."

"Yeah, well, I'd say Diana's right. We both watched Hannah come in hours later than she should have been. No apology, no nothing. She was fuming about something and took it out on Diana before storming off to her office. She totally blanked me. It was as if she didn't recognise me."

How anyone could forget Edna was a mystery to Marjorie. Hannah must have done it deliberately.

"I agree with you that Hannah doesn't have the people skills one would expect from someone in her position. Her conversation is monosyllabic, but I don't think that, or her being late today, is enough to accuse her of wrongdoing."

"You and Horace need to get inside her office," Edna declared.

"Now, just a minute! I don't think that's a good idea," said Frederick.

"Nothing's ever a good idea with you, but it's the best way of finding out more about Hannah McMighty and what she's up to."

"If anything," retorted Frederick.

"Edna has a point," said Horace. "We have to start somewhere because it feels like we're going round in circles here, and I don't want to stay a moment longer than necessary, no matter what I said to Sergeant Frame. I vote we do it, and while we're at it, we'll check Ruby's office."

"And Pete's," said Edna.

"Why Pete's?" Frederick looked aghast. "Surely these people are entitled to some privacy."

"Eleanor told me some of the others think that there is something suspicious about Jackie's and Carl's deaths, and that he's behind it all. I don't believe it and to be honest, she could have been confused about what people are saying. She doesn't always hear properly, but we might as well rule some of them out as well as in."

"But what are you looking for? A written confession?" Frederick had paled.

"That would be nice," said Marjorie, chuckling, "but we might uncover something pointing towards a motive. The staff appear to keep paper records because Hannah had a file on me. It would be perfect if we could take a peek at Carl and Jackie's notes."

"Right. We'll do it tonight," said Horace, determined.

"I could sneak back and help," offered Edna.

"That's not a good idea," said Horace. "I'll phone you once we're done."

Edna's shoulders dropped along with her mouth.

"You could help, though," Marjorie suggested.

"How?"

"By telling us the nightly routine. I assume there's someone on duty during the night?"

"Yes. They have one person on duty and two on-call."

"Where is the duty person stationed?"

"There's a small office next to Ruby's. Apparently, she won't let them use hers at night in case they eat curry or something."

"Or she could be hiding something," said Horace.

"Or that. Anyway, the night nurse – it's always a qualified nurse – uses an office akin to a cubbyhole. There's a small television in there and every room has two buzzers, one for emergencies and another to call for non-urgent assistance."

"Yes, Diana showed me those yesterday," said Marjorie.

"Anyway, the latter fires off a bleeper the nurse on duty carries."

"And where are the keys to the other offices kept?" Marjorie asked.

"They hang up inside the medicines room, which has a key-coded entry system. I don't know the code. Horace could ask his friend the manager, if he's not in on it."

"I don't think I dare do that. As far as I know, he's still in the Middle East and even if he wasn't, it would be a breach of protocol and confidentiality. He wouldn't agree to it."

"And neither should he."

"I think the code's written on the back of the staff's lanyards because I've seen them checking them before entering the medicines room. There's a spare lanyard hanging on a hook in the cubbyhole in case anyone goes off sick."

Marjorie was impressed at Edna's observation skills. "That's how we get the keys," she declared.

"I've said it before, Marjorie" – Horace chuckled – "you'd make a formidable criminal if ever you decided to switch over to the dark side."

"Not without us, she wouldn't," said Edna, petulantly. "I forgot to tell you, Fred; you can't come to the funeral tomorrow. Diana's bringing Eleanor."

Frederick seemed pleased at the news. He and Edna had worked together on investigations in the past, but Marjorie's cousin-in-law was too forceful for him.

"That's fine. I'll see what I can find out about the staff from their social media accounts."

"Is that information public?" Marjorie quizzed.

"It depends on their privacy settings, but most people drop something about themselves which can give you clues to follow."

"Like breadcrumbs?"

"Precisely. And if their friends' list is public, there's usually one or two that aren't afraid of baring all to the world."

"What a dreadful thought," said Marjorie. "But it's an excellent idea."

"In the meantime, we'll settle down for the evening and catch a nap," said Horace. "I suspect it might be a long night." He winked at Marjorie.

"Come to my room at midnight. Hopefully, everyone will be settled by then," said Marjorie.

Edna shook her head, unable to keep a smirk off her face. "Not if there's a late-night film in the cinema room. I'd make it later if I were you."

"They didn't show me a cinema room," said Marjorie.

"Nor me," said Horace. "But then, I didn't get a proper tour."

"It's a recent addition and is supposed to be for the apartment residents, but a few of the longer-term rehabbers found out about it, and believe me, they use it. I've been there."

"I'll give you a knock at about 2am then," said Horace.

"What about Darren?" Frederick asked. "Don't you think we should take note of Victor's suspicions?"

"I do," said Marjorie. "But I'd really like to sneak a peek at the dead residents' files and look at what's going on with the books. Did I mention Cook's husband is an accountant and is often called in to fix errors?"

Her three friends stared back at her.

"So much happened today, I didn't get the opportunity to mention it. I'll tell you more tomorrow. I think for now, Horace and I need to get some sleep."

Edna didn't argue, but left, shaking her head. Frederick left in a separate car to keep up the charade.

Marjorie headed up to her room, tired but convinced she wouldn't get a wink of sleep with what she and Horace would be doing in the early hours. She wasn't sure what would happen if they were caught and couldn't imagine DS Frame being so friendly if she found out. Marjorie could only hope that wouldn't happen.

TWENTY-FOUR

As the clock struck two, Marjorie could not sit, instead pacing her room, waiting for the expected tap at the door. She had been dressed and ready for an hour, having given up trying to nap ages ago. Marjorie grew more agitated when fifteen minutes passed and Horace still hadn't arrived.

It was no use. She couldn't wait any longer. She didn't dare use the phone in the room in case it went through some sort of operator, so she opted for her mobile. If only she could remember where she'd put it.

Marjorie ran through the day she'd unpacked her belongings in her mind, but couldn't recall putting the wretched thing away. Lectures from Jeremy and Edna replayed in her mind as she rifled through drawers. She wracked her brains until she remembered Edna's phone call on Monday. Of course!

"It's in your handbag, silly." Marjorie reached for the handbag on the bedside table and took the phone out. Was it really just three days since her monthly hairdressing outing had been interrupted? She tried switching the phone on, but nothing happened.

"What's the matter with you?" She shook it as if doing so

would spark it into life. Still nothing. Finally, she remembered that her interfering son had switched it on, which had been the catalyst for her being here in the first place. Marjorie had switched it off, but then back on again to call Frederick on the train journey. She couldn't have switched it off again.

She opened her handbag wide, tipping everything onto the bed, but realised it was a hopeless case. The charger was sitting in a drawer at home in Hampstead!

Marjorie checked her watch again. It was now quarter to three. Horace must have fallen asleep, or perhaps the night nurse had been called to his floor. In either case, she should get moving.

Deciding it would be less suspicious if anyone saw her wandering around the home in the middle of the night, she changed back into a nightgown and dressing gown, plus slippers. Dim night lighting helped her navigate her way to the ground floor. Marjorie kept to the edges of the building as she made her way towards Ruby's office and beyond. She needed to know if the night nurse was in their office before risking what she was about to do.

Taking slow steps towards the room Edna had described as a cubbyhole, she could see the door was slightly ajar and light filtered out onto the cream carpet. Although she was annoyed with Horace for not turning up, her determination was more resolute than normal. The glass window to the office was frosted and she couldn't see inside. She could hear low voices and soon realised the television was on.

Stooping down so as not to reveal her shadow through the frosted glass, Marjorie tiptoed towards the door. Her pounding heart sounded as loud as the television. She had to get inside the room to grab that lanyard.

Barely breathing, she pushed the door an inch, sending a silent prayer heavenward that it wouldn't creak. It didn't. With no reaction to her trial run, Marjorie pushed it open further until there was enough space to poke her head around the door to see inside. As she did so, Marjorie rehearsed an excuse for being there if the nurse saw her.

All she could see was a head of multicoloured hair facing away from the door towards the television. The show was a comedy, and every so often, the person guffawed in a manner similar to Edna. There was a desk in front of the turned-away chair where Marjorie could see a maroon notebook. To the left was a hook with not one, but two lanyards hanging. Marjorie placed one foot in front of the other, wishing again that Horace was here because he would have been able to reach it without entering the room.

Just as she reached for the first lanyard, Marjorie felt her heart was going to explode as the chair shifted. Another joke drew the nurse's attention back to the screen and Marjorie took advantage of an extra loud guffaw, grabbing the lanyard and stepping out of the room. No sooner was she outside than she lost her footing, tripping over something. Timmy's meow was loud enough to draw the attention of the person inside and Marjorie ducked behind a large parlour palm.

"Oh, it's you, Timmy. Come on then, you can sit with me. I've got a tin of sardines you'll love." The nurse closed the door after Timmy and Marjorie released the breath she had been holding for what felt like an eternity.

"No wonder Cook's going to give that cat a weekly weigh-in," she muttered.

"Weigh in. Weigh in." Marjorie's heart almost stopped again, but when she looked at Apollo's cage, it was covered and his words were only just audible to her ears.

Turning away from the waiting room and the foyer, Marjorie moved back into the shadows and flipped the lanyard, hoping to find the code she was looking for using the light from one of the night lamps. Edna was right.

Marjorie found the keys hanging up inside the medicines

room and left the lanyard in there, hoping that when the morning came, the staff would think someone had put it there by mistake. Another thirty minutes had passed since she left her room and the nurse might decide to do a round or a call bell might sound at any moment. Marjorie had no time to waste. Some people would be very early risers and might start exploring the place for themselves.

Despite Edna's fixation with Hannah, Marjorie wanted to start with Ruby Haigh's office before moving into the staff corridor. It also made sense that she would be less likely to be discovered if she started nearest to the cubbyhole and finished as far away as possible. Treading cautiously around Apollo's cage and checking the cubbyhole door was still closed, Marjorie was pleased to find labelled tags attached to the keys. With a trembling hand, she inserted the key into the administrator's lock and turned. The click sounded unnecessarily loud in the early hours of the morning. She heard a word coming from behind the parrot's blanket that made her wonder if someone in the home had been undoing the good work of his former Quaker owners.

Once in the office, Marjorie closed the door and locked it from the inside. There was a little light coming in from the outside lamps, but not enough for the task at hand. With a heavy sigh and another silent prayer, Marjorie closed the Venetian blind and switched the light on. If she was quick, she could be in and out without the night nurse being any the wiser. She didn't like to contemplate what would happen if the nurse caught her.

After opening a few drawers, Marjorie found what she was looking for. She perused the pages as well as she could, but realised that it was only Frederick or Horace that could interpret what was inside. If her mobile phone had been charged, she would have been able to take photos, but as it was...

"Ah, that might help." Marjorie spied the photocopier and

started to make copies of the most recent entries, hoping the nurse still had the television volume up as loud as it had been or she would catch her at any moment. Cook had mentioned that her husband was only called in when there were anomalies in the accounts. Ten pages was all she dared copy before replacing the book.

She sat for a moment in Ruby's chair, checking around the office, and then examined the desk itself. It was tidy and organised as she would expect from the efficient Ruby Haigh. The in-tray contained letters addressed to the home, many of which were referrals from outside. Resisting the temptation to check whether any related to her or Horace, Marjorie flicked through each one until she came to a name she recognised. Her eyes narrowed as she read and she felt anger searing through her with each paragraph.

When she heard a light tap at the door, she dropped all the papers on the floor. Her eyes flicked around the room, looking for an escape route. Then she heard a whisper from behind the door.

"Marjorie, are you in there?"

She quickly unlocked the door, returned to the desk, and picked the papers up before replacing them inside the in-tray, hoping they were in some sort of order, but doubting it very much.

"Where were you?"

Horace brought his fingers to his mouth. "Not here."

The two of them left the office, making as little noise as possible, and Marjorie locked the door. They had just unlocked the entrance to the staff corridor when they heard a van pull up outside. Holding the door slightly open, Marjorie could not believe her eyes when she saw a person she recognised sneak inside the care home and head to the night nurse's office.

"That was close. They almost caught us. Who is that?" asked Horace, peering over Marjorie's shoulder.

"Hannah McManus, the physiotherapist."

"What's she doing here at this time of night?"

"That's what I'd like to know. After what I found in Ruby's office just now, I was about to call this whole fiasco off, but now I'm not so sure. I assume the answer to the question might lie in these."

Marjorie held up the rolled-up bunch of photocopies she'd tucked inside her dressing gown pocket.

TWENTY-FIVE

Marjorie and Horace stood frozen, their eyes glued to the small opening she'd created in the doorway. Her heart quickened and she was unable to move her gaze away from the disturbing scene unfolding before them.

"No wonder she was so late into work today with all of this going on at night. I can't believe this sort of thing is happening under Pete's nose," Marjorie whispered.

"It looks like they're bringing in a delivery," said Horace.

"In the middle of the night?"

"Do you think it's a robbery?" Horace asked.

Marjorie felt her head nod. "It's got to be some kind of theft."

"But they're bringing stuff in rather than taking it out," Horace argued.

In the dim light, they watched Hannah, a male accomplice, and the night nurse carry around twenty cartons from the waiting van. The trio moved with a sense of urgency and caution, all in complete silence. Hannah's hand gestures and whispers conveyed an impression of careful planning as she pointed to a door next to the medicines room. As they disappeared through the door, it closed silently behind them.

Intrigued by the mysterious activity, Marjorie and Horace remained motionless. "It's like watching a heist in reverse," she whispered.

The minutes ticked by slowly as the intruders remained concealed from view. After what felt like an eternity, but was only twenty minutes, the night nurse returned and shut the front doors. She nervously scanned her surroundings before pacing back and forth with hushed steps. Every so often, the nurse returned to the door where Hannah and her accomplice remained out of sight, popped her head around, and then moved back to the front door to keep watch. She ignored Timmy when he wound himself round her legs, his purrs breaking through the silence of the night.

"Not now, Timmy," she muttered.

Horace pulled the door to the corridor closed, and he and Marjorie waited once more, ears to the door.

"You haven't told me why you were so late."

"Sorry about that. I drank a mug of hot chocolate and must have nodded off in the chair."

"Are you sure the drink wasn't spiked with something?"

"I doubt it. Why would anyone do that?"

"I'm not sure, but considering you found Victor this morning and have been asking a lot of questions, and in view of what's happening here, it's possible that someone might want to keep you out of the way."

"Why would they drug me and not you?"

"I only drank tap water after returning to my room."

"If somebody spiked my drink, it had to be Hannah."

"It could be nothing and I'm being neurotic. Victor Redman has a lot to answer for."

"Good idea you putting on nightwear, by the way. I didn't even get undressed."

"Shush, I hear movement." Marjorie opened the door a couple of inches. It was the nurse letting Timmy out through the front entrance. She then crossed the room and kept watch at the foot of the stairs.

"I wonder what they're up to in there," said Horace.

"Theft of some sort. She looks nervous," said Marjorie.

"So she should be. Looks like you were right, Marjorie. Here they come again."

This time, they watched the three carrying the same twenty cartons out to the van, but more slowly.

"Those cartons are full now. I've seen enough. Close the door," said Marjorie.

"What now?"

"We call the police and tell them they haven't got long to get here."

"Right," said Horace.

Marjorie opened the nearest office door, which happened to be Hannah McManus's. Horace hurried to the phone while Marjorie watched the trio reload the van through the window.

"Police... Yes... Hello, I'm calling from Evergreen Acres Retirement Homes & Rehabilitation Centre. There's a robbery in progress. Yes, that's what I said. The culprits are loading a van as we speak. You need to come quickly. Pardon? My name?" Horace checked with Marjorie, who shook her head. "Sorry, someone's coming. Be quick." Horace placed the phone back on its base. "Before I cut them off, they said they would send a car."

"I think they're going to be too late. This lot work fast. Do you have a camera with you?"

"Better than that, I can video with this thing." Horace used his phone to shoot a video from behind the window. Nobody was looking their way. They were too busy loading their heist.

A few minutes later, Hannah climbed into the passenger

seat. The doors of the van were quietly closed and the driver drove into the night. All was quiet again.

"Did you get a shot of her?" Marjorie asked.

"Yes, and the driver and number plate. They won't get far."

"Good," said Marjorie. "While we're here, let's see what she's got to hide."

"First, let me take photos of those papers you've got and send Fred a message. He might save us some time and give the police a heads up."

Marjorie handed the photocopies to Horace, and then began opening and closing drawers, finding nothing. "She's at least got the good sense not to leave anything incriminating in here."

Horace's mobile burst into life, making them both jump.

"It's Fred."

"Put him on speaker. The nurse will be back in that office. She won't hear us from there."

"Hello, Fred, you're on speaker, but keep your voice down. We're safe, but don't want to attract attention," said Horace.

"Are you sure it's okay to talk?"

"Yes, we're fine," said Marjorie. "We've just watched Hannah McManus shifting boxes in and out of the home. Do those images tell you anything?"

"Two things jump out, but I would need more time to examine them properly."

"What are the two things?" Marjorie asked.

"It looks like whoever is keeping the books is questioning certain high-value expenses. They've put a question mark next to them. This is usually done when there's a lack of supporting documentation, such as invoices or receipts, and is suggesting the transactions might be fabricated to siphon funds."

"Ruby keeps the books, and I think I mentioned Cook told me her husband is called in to explain things when Ruby gets in a muddle."

"Which could mean he's in on it, if there is something going wrong there. It might also mean someone's lost the paperwork," said Frederick.

"What was the second thing?"

"This one's more of a red flag. Quite a few of the entries are not in chronological order. Someone – Hannah, from what you've just said – has manipulated the order of transactions to hide specific expenses, which means she's siphoning off supplies and maybe selling them elsewhere. It will be easier to trace with Hannah under the spotlight. They'll be able to pinpoint what she's doing."

"Thank you, Frederick."

"Carl and Jackie must have worked out what Hannah was doing, and she killed them for it," said Horace.

"I don't think so," said Marjorie. "Is Edna with you, Frederick?"

"No, she's fast asleep. I can hear her snoring in the next room. Do you want me to wake her?"

"No. It can wait until tomorrow. I can hear a car. We called the police. Hopefully that's them arriving."

"They took their time," said Horace. "See you in the morning, Fred."

"Right. I'll try to get a few hours' sleep, then. I've been waiting for you to call."

"Goodnight," Marjorie and Horace spoke in unison before he put the phone back inside his pocket.

They closed Hannah's office door behind them as they left and opened the door from the staff corridor, noticing the night nurse was refusing to let the police inside the building. She was holding the entrance door ajar.

"I don't know what you're talking about. Somebody is playing tricks on you. Most likely a hoax. It's been quiet all night. I think you should go before you wake any of the residents."

Marjorie grabbed Horace's arm, whispering, "You go. I'll head back to bed because I don't believe Hannah is responsible for the attack on Victor, so we don't want to play all our cards at once."

"But—"

"She's a thief, but I don't believe she's a killer. I'll explain in the morning. Please distract them so that I can sneak upstairs. Tell them you couldn't sleep or something."

Horace handed back the photocopies, and she put them in her dressing gown pocket. Marjorie watched as Horace circled behind the commotion at the door and approached from a different direction.

"Good evening, Officers. I'm the person who made the telephone call. I can assure you it's not a hoax."

As every head turned to look at Horace, Marjorie closed the corridor door, turned the key in the lock, and moved into the shadows.

"Who are you?" the nurse shouted.

"The name's Horace Tyler. I think you should invite the officers inside so that we can talk. Mustn't keep them out there in the cold."

"Well, I, er—"

"It will be better if we go somewhere quiet, Nurse," said a broad-shouldered policeman, taking advantage of her confusion and stepping inside.

"Let's hear what Mr Tyler has to say, shall we?" said the other officer.

"I have to do my rounds."

"Don't fall for that one, Officer. This young lady is involved in a crime that took place not so long ago."

"Don't be ridiculous! I think this man's delusional."

Marjorie couldn't resist a quiet giggle while she watched the nurse trying to squirm her way out of the situation, totally unaware of how much Horace had witnessed.

She waited for the party to move into the lounge before, thankful she was able to recall the code, she returned the keys to the medicines room. By the time she got back to her own room, she was breathless and excited. Things were falling into place. There were just a few more pieces of the puzzle to unravel.

TWENTY-SIX

Marjorie opened the door to find Cook standing there, holding a tray of food.

"Do come inside. I didn't expect you to bring it. I do hope I haven't put you to any trouble."

Cook's usually bright eyes were filled with worry. "It's no trouble at all. We're overrun with agency staff this morning. The regulars have been called in to an urgent meeting with the chief exec."

"Oh dear. Has something happened?"

"I probably shouldn't say anything, but word will get around soon enough." Cook put the tray down on a table. Marjorie was pleased to see the requested phone charger, along with a hearty breakfast and a pot of tea. "I can hardly believe it. Hannah and one of the night nurses have been arrested. Your new friend, Horace Tyler, caught them stealing in the middle of the night."

"Stealing? That's terrible."

"Even if Horace hadn't caught them at it, they would have been exposed today. My Eric tells me he's suspected it's been going on for some time. He'd asked Ruby to highlight anything that appeared odd in the books, and he's been checking the discrepancies. He'd already worked out Hannah was up to no good and was coming in today to explain his theory to Ruby and the CEO. Now Horace has witnessed her taking stuff, it will be a lot easier to get a conviction. I doubt the owners are pleased about it, though. They hate adverse publicity, so I expect they would have just sacked her. Still, best that people get what they deserve."

"I never would have imagined anything underhand going on in a place like this," said Marjorie, deep in thought.

"It just goes to show. Anyway, I'll let you get on with your breakfast. I've got most of the kitchen staff arriving in the next hour. We'll make sure people are fed and watered, don't you worry. I almost forgot to tell you. Pete asked me to apologise and let you know they cancelled your physio session today."

Marjorie inwardly whooped, saying, "Such a shame, but I understand there are more important things going on at present. Perhaps I'll go for a walk instead."

"Walking's far more enjoyable than being in that gym, no matter how fancy the equipment is. That's what I always say to my Eric. Enjoy your breakfast, Marjorie."

"Thank you." Marjorie grinned as the door closed. She had just poured tea when she heard another knock. Had Cook forgotten something?

She was delighted to see Horace when she opened the door. "I wasn't sure whether you would be up," he said, "but I saw Cook and she told me she'd just brought you breakfast. I waited until she was out of sight. Didn't want to start any rumours." Horace laughed, but thankfully omitted the usual snort he and Edna shared.

"Come on in, Cook's brought enough breakfast to feed three people! There's a mug over by the kettle if you'd like tea, or there are coffee sachets."

"I'll make a coffee," said Horace. "I could do with the caffeine."

Once they were both settled in easy chairs and Horace had helped himself to the four slices of toast from the rack, lathering them with butter and marmalade. Marjorie let him eat before breaking the easy silence.

"Cook's already told me the nurse and Hannah have been arrested. What else have you got to add?"

Horace finished his last mouthful of toast, wiped his mouth and began. "The nurse tried to deny everything at first, but once I showed her, and the police, the video, she caved. They've also got CCTV footage from outside which she hadn't had the time to delete. DS Frame arrived at about 5am to say that Hannah and her accomplice were being questioned at the station and the police had retrieved all the stolen goods."

"Who is the accomplice?"

"The nurse's partner, Alan something or other. Her name's Shelly. She'd been an unwilling party, bullied into getting involved by him, poor girl. He's known to the police and has a history as a loan shark and other criminal activities. It turns out Hannah's husband has racked up gambling debts to the tune of thousands, and then borrowed from this man at an extortionate rate of interest. Scum of the Earth, these people, taking advantage of others' weaknesses. Anyway, this Alan guy threatened to do Hannah's husband serious harm if he didn't repay him. It wasn't long before Alan, knowing about Hannah from his partner, forced them into this little side hustle. It started small, but got bigger and bigger, and of course, because the interest on the loan was so high—"

"The debt was never paid. I almost feel sorry for the poor woman, but why didn't she and her husband tell someone about it?"

Horace shook his head. "Hannah was too ashamed, plus the

guy had threatened what he would do to them if either of them did, and Shelly was the browbeaten girlfriend of a brute."

"I hope the authorities take that into account," said Marjorie.

"I'm sure the law will, but the nurse regulator might not go too easy on her. I doubt she'll ever work as a nurse again."

"And Hannah will go to prison."

"While her husband gets off," said Horace.

"How?"

"Because they have young children, and Hannah insists he didn't know about any of this. The DS doesn't believe her, but while she maintains her story, her husband has deniability."

"I hope she's doing the right thing for the children. Gambling addiction is a hard habit to break."

"According to DS Frame, he's agreed to seek help for the children's sake."

"That's something, I suppose."

"Anyway, the DS believes Victor found out about their little scheme and Hannah or the nurse is responsible for drugging him. She said she'll come back to us on that one."

"Hmm."

"You don't think either of them got to Victor, do you?"

"What makes you say that?"

"The look on your face, plus you more or less said so earlier."

Marjorie had been cogitating since returning to her room and felt much clearer about the next plan of action. "You're quite right. I don't, but I must speak to DS Frame about something. I'm going to need your support."

"I might regret this, but you've got it."

"Did I tell you that Edna's friend, Carl, died from a burst aortic aneurysm?"

"No. Is that what you meant when you said you'd been about to call everything off last night?"

"It was actually this morning, but I know what you mean," said Marjorie. "Yes, it was. I found a detailed letter from a hospital consultant, warning that the aneurysm was inoperable and that the poor man could die suddenly at any moment. There was also a letter from Dr Branson, detailing her examination post-mortem, which fitted with the symptoms of a burst aneurysm and she certified the death accordingly."

"I thought Edna said he was fit and worked out?"

"He must have lied to Edna. The letter made it quite clear Carl didn't want his diagnosis to be discussed with anyone outside of his medical team. He didn't even tell his family."

"Which points to them both dying from natural causes, so DS Frame's theory that Victor worked out what Hannah and the nurse were up to makes sense. Why do you doubt it?"

"I thought the same initially, but we still don't have enough information about Jackie's death, or the reason Victor was rooting around in the empty apartments. If it was Hannah's crimes he'd been concerned with, he would have spoken to Pete."

"I'm not quite following, but go on."

"Victor didn't sleep well, Isabelle told me that, and he often stood at his window watching things, with a full view of the main entrance. He would have known what Hannah was up to for some time and I hate to say this, but I suspect Hannah paid him to keep quiet."

"He blackmailed her, you mean?"

Marjorie shrugged. "Either that, or knowing his habits, she offered him money for his silence."

"So Victor might have had the murky background you and Isabelle suspected?"

Marjorie let out an enormous sigh. "I think so. We don't know the pressure he was under for all those years in the police force, and I expect the divorce took its toll on him. It might have been anger that pushed him to break the law and help himself to something he might consider as reward for his service."

"It's still wrong and you know how Fred will feel about it."

Marjorie was well aware how Frederick saw things in black and white. "I'm not condoning his behaviour. I'm trying to understand it."

"If your theory is right, Victor was prepared to turn a blind eye, even profit from theft or fraud, but not to murder."

"Hence his anger at anyone being cleared by the courts."

"Such as Darren."

"Exactly. And I still believe, rightly or wrongly, he suspected Darren killed his bridge friend, Jackie Bagshaw, and was getting away with murder twice." Marjorie removed the charger from the tray and plugged her phone in. "We need to call the police station."

"No need," said Horace, holding up his phone. "DS Frame gave me her mobile number in case I remembered anything else."

"Do you think you could persuade her to come here? I'd rather do this face-to-face."

TWENTY-SEVEN

The detective sergeant hadn't been alone when she visited Marjorie and, while she listened patiently and asked pertinent questions, her DI had been far less accommodating. He had rolled his eyes too often in Marjorie's opinion and, if it hadn't been for DS Frame, wouldn't have stayed long enough to hear all her concerns. The two detectives had left saying they would consider what Marjorie had suggested, but could make no promises, which infuriated her.

"We should go for a walk," Horace suggested. "It might calm you down."

"He didn't have to be so condescending. I don't believe for one minute he'll act on any of our suspicions. He's convinced he's got Victor's attacker and as for anything else, he's not interested."

"But DS Frame was listening. Maybe she'll be able to talk sense into him. Although he could be right, you know."

Marjorie was aware she might be wrong, but what if she wasn't? There wouldn't be another opportunity.

"We should look inside Victor's apartment for ourselves. He

had a pile of papers on the table in his front room, which hasn't sat comfortably with me."

"Did you notice the way the DI scowled whenever we talked about Victor?"

"Yes, I did. He knows something, most likely confirming our suspicions that Victor did something wrong in the past. That doesn't mean Victor was wrong about his friend."

"Didn't he also go into Carl's apartment? If he thought he was murdered, he was wrong about that."

"I know, but that might have been a matter of routine. Two sudden deaths roused his suspicions. Remember, Carl kept his aneurysm a secret."

"There is another theory," said Horace, eyeing Marjorie cautiously.

"I know what you're going to say, and I don't believe it. If he took money, it was only from criminals. He wouldn't have robbed his friends."

"A modern day Robin Hood," Horace chortled.

This conversation wasn't helping Marjorie's stress levels, and it certainly wasn't calming her anger. "Are you coming or not?"

"How will we get in?"

"If the crime scene investigators haven't left the door open for us, we'll go around the back."

Horace didn't seem as keen as he would normally. He believed she was wrong, which was disconcerting. Marjorie wondered whether to concede defeat, but whatever wrongs Victor had done in his past, he didn't deserve to be lying in a hospital bed because of trying to hunt down a killer. The DI had scoffed at her when she suggested he might have known what Hannah was up to for months, and taken money to turn a blind eye, but the look on DS Frame's face told her she had struck a chord with her. It was that which motivated her to follow her instincts, rather than give up.

"Okay, let's go. I haven't been able to get hold of Edna this morning. I expect she's on her way to the funeral and put her phone on silent."

When Marjorie and Horace pretend-met downstairs, the atmosphere was one of tension with hushed conversations taking place as people sat in small huddles. Word was out, and older people – in fact, most people – love nothing more than a good gossip. What had transpired would keep them going for days, and would do far more for them than any rehabilitation programme. Marjorie couldn't resist sticking her tongue out at the gymnasium on the way past. Horace tried to hide a smirk.

"One thing's certain, I won't be going in there again," said Marjorie. "Whatever the outcome, I'd like to be out of this place by tomorrow."

Horace rubbed his left eye. "Me too. Those saline drops might be harmless, but they're making my eye sore. One of the agency nurses caught me before I came to your room earlier."

Once outside, the two of them discovered the turning circle was almost empty. The police car had long gone, and the cordon was no longer surrounding Victor's apartment. They strolled casually along, having a quick look around before turning on to the path that led to his front door.

"Good. They haven't got around to fixing it yet," said Marjorie.

Horace pushed the door open and stood back to allow her inside first. Almost as soon as he closed it, they heard shuffling noises coming from the front room.

Marjorie put a finger to her lips and tiptoed forwards with Horace keeping in step. They both peered around the door frame at the same time.

"What are you doing?" Marjorie asked, surprised.

Isabelle looked up, startled. "I was clearing things."

Horace was as confused as Marjorie, judging by the lines on

his forehead. Marjorie kept her eyes on Isabelle's, challenging her.

Isabelle flopped into an easy chair. "I just got a call from the hospital." Tears flooded down her face.

"I'm so sorry," said Marjorie.

Horace was at Isabelle's side in an instant, pulling another chair close and holding her hand. "If there's anything we can do."

Isabelle shook her head, dabbing her eyes with a handkerchief. "This was his favourite chair."

"You were very fond of him, weren't you?" Marjorie said.

"I was, but he wasn't all good."

"Something you had in common, I suspect."

Horace's eyes opened wide, but Marjorie kept hers on Isabelle.

"Like he said, you're very perceptive, Marjorie. I suppose it doesn't matter now, but yes, I knew he had siphoned criminal money from raids and squirrelled it away. That's how he could afford to live here."

"But surely you didn't do him harm?" Horace asked.

"Certainly not!" Isabelle snapped. "He was my friend, and he deserved a bit of comfort in his old age. His pension wouldn't have been enough to cover all this. But I'm no saint. We shared things about our past, that's all. One night we'd both had a lot to drink. We went into confessional mode. He hadn't been to confession for over forty years, so he told me about the dirty money he'd hidden away over the years. When he retired, he dug it up and moved here. He felt terribly guilty, so to make him feel better, I told him about something I have regretted all my working life."

Marjorie patted her hand. "And you believe he might have written it down somewhere. Is that what you're looking for now?"

Isabelle nodded. "Not at first. I came here to hide from my

grief and feel a little bit closer to him. It's only when I saw the papers, I wondered. He still carried a notebook around in his pocket, even after all these years."

"I'm afraid someone else, before the crime scene investigators, has already been through his papers and notebooks, but they wouldn't have been looking for the same thing you were. I don't believe he would have written your secret. To his friends, he remained loyal."

"I think you're right. It's why I ushered you out of here yesterday, just in case he had, but I should have realised someone else had been here."

"So you weren't entirely honest when you said he was a private person and that you didn't come in here," Marjorie said.

"He was a private person. That part was true. After that night of drunken confessions, neither of us ever spoke about what we'd shared again. It was as if we flicked a switch on our memories, silently agreeing not to discuss the matter."

"What is it that's burdened you for so long?" Horace asked.

"The article that launched my career. I plagiarised it." Isabelle sobbed quietly into the hankie.

"Who from?" Marjorie asked.

"Before working for *Vogue*, I worked for a minor fashion magazine. An admin assistant had an argument with the editorial director and stormed out of the office. As a junior, I was given her desk and told to clear it out myself. In the drawer, I found a handwritten article and was impressed with it. I typed it up and submitted it to the editor. A week later, I was given my first big interview on the back of that article."

"Did the writer of the piece ever try to contact you?" Horace asked.

"No, but I should have put her name to it. Although, if I recall correctly, she hadn't put her name to it either."

Marjorie felt empathy for both women. "Would the article

have been published in her name if you had shown it to the editor?"

Isabelle shook her head. "I doubt she'd have even looked at it, and even if she had, the woman wouldn't have been credited. Not after the row. The magazine owned everything we wrote, anyway. We just got credited."

"We've all done things we regret in life," said Marjorie cautiously. "Whilst I don't condone what you did, I fear you've carried this guilt for far too long. If you hadn't been good at what you did, you wouldn't have gone as far as you did in your career."

"I agree with Marjorie," said Horace. "There's a case for going back and righting what you did wrong with the person who wrote the article, but I don't think you should treat your entire career as a sham over that one misdemeanour. If it hadn't been credited to you, it would have been credited to your editor or the magazine. In my business, it happens all the time. One of our scientists gets an idea for a component and if we're not careful, by the time it's produced, someone else has come up with the same thing. Nowadays, the company is a lot savvier with airtight patents, but back in the day, that sort of thing was commonplace. Without a patent, it's a free for all, and even with one, people can develop something near enough the same. I expect it's like that with copyright. People can steal your ideas even if they don't replicate your work."

Isabelle dried her eyes. "Thank you for being so understanding. I've lived with this burden for far too long and you're right. I was very good at what I did."

"I take it you heard about Hannah's arrest," said Marjorie.

"Yes, I did. Do you think she was the one who killed Victor?"

Marjorie shook her head. "No. Victor was on to something in relation to Jackie Bagshaw's death. I don't suppose you found any of his notes regarding that?"

"There are pages torn out of his most recent notebook." Isabelle reached behind her and handed the book to Marjorie.

Marjorie scanned it. "The pages are dated, and the ones missing are from the day they found Jackie dead. Prior to that, he noted nothing about Carl's death as being odd."

Horace frowned. "You could be right that Jackie's death was the catalyst for him to investigate further. But why didn't he investigate Carl's death after Jackie told him she thought she'd be next?"

"I have a theory about that. Victor wasn't known for his warmth, maybe he didn't care about Carl and imagined Jackie was overreacting."

"But obviously Jackie suspected something or she wouldn't have been frightened," Isabelle said.

"Either that or Carl's death triggered her own sense of mortality. Perhaps she had an underlying illness nobody was aware of."

"But Victor did find something, or the pages wouldn't have been torn out," said Horace.

"Precisely," said Marjorie.

"Surely you don't think he was right and that Darren had something to do with her death?" Isabelle said.

"That's what we're going to find out. Do you mind if I take this?"

"If it helps you discover who did this to Victor, take whatever you like."

"And please don't mention this conversation to anyone else. As far as the police are concerned, Hannah drugged Victor."

Isabelle's eyes filled up again. "His daughter refused to visit him. How could she do that?"

Marjorie sighed. "I really am sorry for your loss."

TWENTY-EIGHT

There were very few people standing outside of the crematorium chapel when Edna got there. She double-checked the list of services for the day and noted she was in the right place. A couple were smoking cigarettes off to one side. Edna wondered if either was family but didn't like to intrude. If she was being honest, cigarette smoke affected her lungs these days far more than it used to when she sang in clubs and pubs throughout her career.

A queue of eight people had formed by the time she'd used the toilet and arrived back at the chapel. Diana and Eleanor arrived just in time to stand with her as the funeral cortege drove slowly towards the entrance. Eleanor seemed frail and not ready to talk. The effort of getting there had most likely been momentous.

Diana waved to a woman who joined the back of the queue a few minutes later. Once the coffin was taken inside, followed by the people Edna assumed were family, the rest of them trailed into the small chapel. Edna took a chair and picked up the Order of Service. On the front was a photo of a much younger Jackie Bagshaw.

Before she knew what was happening, Edna felt tears rolling down her face. She hadn't known Jackie that well, but seeing a picture of her in her youth reminded Edna that this woman had lived a full and useful life before someone had snatched it away from her. Edna felt slightly guilty about her ulterior motive for being at the funeral, but the sorrow and anger made her even more determined to find out what had happened to her friend.

"Are you okay, Edna?" Diana, who had taken a seat behind her, patted her on the shoulder.

Edna nodded. "Just feeling a bit emotional. She went so suddenly, I wish I'd had the chance to say goodbye."

Diana smiled sympathetically, but was then distracted when the woman who'd joined the back of the queue moments before sat next to her. Edna overheard a few conciliatory words from the woman, who appeared to be in her fifties, along with complimentary sentences about Jackie. Edna reflected on how speech was always stilted at funerals.

Eleanor sat next to Edna, and the women exchanged a light embrace before the service began. During the eulogy, Edna learned Jackie had made her fortune from being an early investor in land and property, had been professionally voice-trained and was a successful tournament tennis player. The last Edna had known about because Jackie had a few trophies on display in her room.

A slide show followed the eulogy with pictures from her childhood, through her entrepreneurial years and finishing with her love for tennis. Many photos included pets, and cats in particular. The cat photos resulted in a few positive murmurs and whispers from the woman sitting next to Diana in the seat behind.

The service ended with the hymn *Abide with Me* while the curtains surrounding the coffin closed. Both Eleanor and Edna choked the words of the hymn out before their tears prevented them from finishing it.

The family had sat in the front row and Eleanor had pointed them out to Edna. They left first with the vicar and waited at the exits to greet people on the way out.

Edna wanted to leave last, so she and Eleanor sat reminiscing about Eleanor's friendship with Jackie.

"I didn't realise she had been a successful businesswoman. I assumed she'd been rich from the word go," said Edna.

"They have all done all right for themselves. Jackie employed her two nephews and handed the property business over to them and her niece when she retired."

"That was generous."

"Jackie promised her brothers she'd take care of them. They both died in their sixties."

Edna was about to ask another question, but Eleanor stood up.

"We'd better go. There'll be another lot in soon."

Eleanor was right, people from another party were already lining up outside. Edna managed a quick hello and thank you to the vicar, but the rest of the funeral party had moved to a designated square of garden to chat or look at the family flowers.

The woman Eleanor had pointed out as Jackie's niece greeted them. "Hello, Eleanor. I'm glad you could make it. Auntie Jackie would have been so pleased."

"Thank you, Mavis. How are you all?"

"The boys are as busy as ever and..." There followed a lengthy description of people Edna assumed were part of Mavis's family circle. There wasn't much mention of Auntie Jackie after the initial opener. It was clear that Mavis's immediate family was foremost in her mind.

"This is Edna. She stayed at Evergreen Acres for a spell of rehab and got on well with Jackie and Carl. We put on a few performances together. You know how your aunt loved to sing."

Mavis shook Edna's hand. "Thank you for coming. Eleanor's right, Auntie Jackie enjoyed performing."

"As well as playing tennis." One of Jackie's nephews, who'd read a poem during the service, joined them.

"This is Keith Bagshaw, my cousin," said Mavis. "Also Auntie Jackie's nephew. He and my brother Mark run the property side of the business now."

"Did I hear my name?" An overweight man with a bald head turned in their direction.

"Eleanor's here with a friend from Evergreen Acres. We were just saying how Auntie Jackie loved singing and playing tennis."

"Not as much as she loved her bloomin' felines. Whenever I visited, we had to take a walk outside. I'm allergic." Mark was now part of their group, as most people had dispersed.

"Speaking of cats, how's Timmy?" Keith asked. "I swear she thought that animal was human."

"He misses her," said Eleanor. "We all do, but Cook is trying to stop us from killing him with kindness."

Keith cackled.

"Had your aunt lived in the home for long?" Edna was enjoying speaking to these three, but felt Marjorie's voice in her head urging her to get on with the job in hand.

"Around ten years. She would have been welcome to stay with any of us, or in one of the multiple properties she owned, but she didn't want to be a burden. It was funny her dying like that. I thought she'd go on for years yet." Keith's eyes changed shades in the noonday sun.

"It was a surprise," Mavis concurred, "but she would have been pleased to bow out quickly with no fuss. I'm just glad she didn't suffer."

"Me too," said Mark. "The old girl's in a better place."

Edna noticed a shared look among the three relatives but couldn't work out whether it was a memory or something more.

Mavis changed the subject. "You're welcome to come back to mine, Eleanor, and you, Edna. We're having a little celebration of Auntie's life."

"That's kind, but Diana's taking me back, and Edna's visiting a friend who's in for rehab."

"Thank you both again for coming."

Edna felt it was time to walk away and leave Jackie's family to speak to Diana and the woman she'd sat with during the service.

"Who is that woman?" Edna asked.

"That's Poppy Peterbald, owner of Poppy's Cat Rescue Centre. Would you believe she has four Peterbalds?"

Edna raised an eyebrow. "What are Peterbalds?"

"Cats, silly. They're really expensive, highly affectionate bald cats."

"Blimey! I'm not sure I'd want a bald cat. How expensive?"

"I think Jackie told me the latest one cost around £1,500. Some things I don't remember, but I'm spot on with numbers."

"Poppy Peterbald's got some dosh, then," said Edna, gloomily.

"She'll have even more now. Jackie's left half of her remaining estate to her."

The news came out of the blue. Edna felt her eyes pop out on stalks. Now, that was a fact Marge would be interested to hear.

TWENTY-NINE

Having gone through the rest of Victor's apartment and finding nothing else, Marjorie was convinced the missing notebook pages would reveal who the true killer was. Horace argued that it could have been Hannah who took them because they incriminated her, but Marjorie knew Hannah's crimes had been going on for longer.

The two images of Victor standing at his front window nagged at her. This, Isabelle confirmed, was something he had been doing ever since she'd met him. That's what convinced Marjorie he would have known what Hannah was up to for ages and was looking the other way, or, more likely, taking money to do so.

Horace checked his watch. "It's almost time for lunch. I don't think we're going to find anything more in here. If there was something, it's gone, along with the pages of that notebook."

Marjorie wasn't ready to give up just yet. "Isabelle? Do you have a key to Jackie's apartment?"

"Yes, but—"

"We could be in and out in ten minutes," said Horace.

Marjorie was grateful he had taken the baton and was offering his support.

"I suppose it won't do any harm. They haven't started clearing it yet."

"Good. Then there's no time like the present." Marjorie put an arm through Isabelle's.

As soon as Isabelle opened the door to Jackie's apartment, Timmy swept past them and ran inside.

"He used to get his lunch around about this time," Isabelle explained.

Jackie's apartment had a similar homely feel to Isabelle's, apart from the cat hairs on the furniture and the bed. The three of them checked papers and letters in Jackie's sideboard, but only found ordinary correspondence. There was a cheque book with stubs, revealing a generous donation to Poppy's Cat Rescue Centre dated the day before Jackie died. Marjorie flicked through the other stubs and found entries of large monthly donations to the cat rescue and a few personal ones made out to Poppy Peterbald.

"Who's Poppy Peterbald?" Marjorie asked, sensing she already knew the answer.

"She owns Poppy's Cat Rescue Centre," Isabelle replied.

What was it with these name alliterations? First the Cook, Patsy Prindle, and now Poppy Peterbald.

"Jackie seems to have given Poppy personal money. Do you know what that was for?" Marjorie asked.

"Yes, Poppy loves her namesakes and had seen a litter for sale in the local paper. Jackie wanted her to have some kittens for herself. Poppy pours all her money into the rescue centre."

"I see," said Marjorie. Other cheques were made out to a tennis centre, and a retired musicians' charity. Nothing out of the ordinary.

While Marjorie continued going through the sideboard,

Horace went into the kitchen. "Nothing in here but tins of cat food and snacks," he called.

"Jackie liked energy biscuits when she went walking, or after playing tennis," said Isabelle.

Marjorie sat back in the chair, perusing the room where Isabelle said Jackie had spent most of her time. Unlike Isabelle's walls, which were lined with photos of celebrities, Jackie's were adorned with family photos and a large oil painting of three children with a large ginger cat.

"Is that her family?"

"Yes, she had two brothers. Both died in their sixties. That was the family cat, Ginger."

"Not very original," said Horace, returning to the room.

"Pets back then weren't given ridiculous names like they are nowadays," remarked Isabelle. "Jackie had a happy childhood."

"Did she ever marry?" Horace asked.

"No. She was unusual for our generation and dedicated her life to her business. Her loves were work, tennis and cats."

"In that order?"

"Not necessarily. She gave her business to the children of her brothers after employing them for years. They all visited her regularly, although one of them wouldn't come inside the apartment because of a cat allergy."

Horace chortled, snorting in the process. Marjorie was grateful when his phone rang.

"It's Edna."

"I don't think there's anything odd here," said Marjorie. "Oh! Hang on a minute, what's this?"

Isabelle took the second cheque book Marjorie had picked up and looked at the one unused cheque. It had been crossed through and never torn away from its stub.

"It's nothing," she said, handing it back to Marjorie.

Horace ended his phone call. "Edna's on her way back from

the funeral. She's discovered that Jackie has left half her estate to the Cat Woman."

"Poppy Peterbald?"

"Yes, I think that's what she said."

"Did you know about this?" Marjorie asked Isabelle.

"I knew she was going to leave some money to the cattery, yes. She's already ensured her nephews and niece are set up for life, although I'd assumed they'd get most of what she left. I doubt they mind, though."

"How much money are we talking about?" Horace asked.

"I'm not sure, but her estate would be worth upwards of three million pounds. But if you're suggesting Poppy had anything to do with Jackie's death, you couldn't be more wrong. That woman doesn't have a nasty bone in her body."

"But that amount of money provides a motive," Horace countered. "And money can cause people to do terrible things."

Marjorie was still staring at the unused cheque in her hand. "Let's get some lunch. We'll see what Edna has to say when she gets back."

THIRTY

Edna was speaking so fast, her words were tumbling out of her mouth. Marjorie and Horace had to ask her to slow down at least three times. Frederick looked tired after his nighttime workload and Marjorie was feeling the effects of the night shift herself.

"Keep your voice down, Edna," she said as Edna became more and more animated and argumentative.

"You lot are as bad as Victor was with all your conspiracy theories, and look where that landed him," said Isabelle. "I've had time to think about it, and sometimes the most obvious solution is the truth. Jackie died of a stroke and Hannah drugged Victor, or he couldn't take anymore. And to be frank, neither can I!"

Ignoring Isabelle completely, Edna looked at Marjorie. "What do we do now? We'll never be able to prove Poppy Peterbald killed Jackie. I've just come from the cremation, remember?"

Marjorie exchanged a quick glance with Horace, but didn't want to say anything in front of Isabelle, just in case she turned out to be involved.

"I would like to speak to the beneficiary."

"Great idea, Marge. We'll force her to confess."

"That's not quite what I had in mind," said Marjorie with a sigh.

"If Eleanor hasn't got it wrong, and she might have, because her memory's not as good as it used to be..." Edna put a hand to the brunette wig she had chosen for the funeral.

"Well?" Frederick sounded exasperated.

"If you don't mind, I'd like to get back to tidying Victor's apartment," said Isabelle. "I had enough of this kind of talk from him." Her eyes misted over.

Marjorie felt sorry for her. "At least he won't have to face charges for what he did if he took money from Hannah."

"You're right, Marjorie. I suppose that's the only good thing that's come out of all this. Good luck with your murder chase."

Marjorie watched Isabelle go. Again, she appeared to have aged since the attack on Victor.

"What's up with her?" Edna snapped. "It's not as if he was even nice."

Horace tapped Edna on the arm. "He was to her. They forged a strong friendship, however odd it may seem to us. She was fond of that man. His past just made him more human in her eyes. Besides, they shared—"

"Many happy times here," Marjorie interrupted. She didn't think now was the time to tell Edna about Victor or Isabelle's past misdemeanours. Edna wasn't always the most sympathetic when it came to human frailty. "You were going to say something about Poppy before we were all side-tracked?"

"Yeah. Eleanor reckons she's coming over with the niece, Mavis, to help clear away some of Jackie's things."

"When?"

"After the wake, or whatever it is they are having."

"Why today?"

"Poppy's going on holiday at the weekend. I guess she can afford to now she's going to be stinking rich."

Marjorie nodded thoughtfully. "Okay, we need to act quickly in case DS Frame wasn't able to do what Horace and I asked her to do."

"Which was?" Edna snapped.

"We asked her, and a rather condescending DI, not to allow Jackie's body to be cremated, and to ask the family for permission to carry out a post-mortem."

Frederick raised an eyebrow, looking impressed. "We should have thought of that earlier."

"Well, I hate to interrupt the mutual admiration society," Edna's voice dripped sarcasm, "but I was at the funeral and it went ahead."

"Yes, that was part of the plan. We wanted the funeral to go ahead, but we don't hold out much hope the cremation wouldn't have too, as the detective inspector was so sceptical."

"Incredulous, actually," added Horace.

"So it's important we don't lose our focus," said Marjorie, determined. "Frederick, I wonder if you could contact someone at the cat rescue centre and ask about Poppy's movements on the day Jackie died and the previous evening? We need to establish whether she was anywhere near Evergreen Acres on the day in question. I don't believe she killed Jackie, Edna, but we need to exclude her."

Frederick nodded. "Of course. I'll make some calls and see what I can uncover."

Marjorie turned to Horace. "Perhaps you and Edna could have a chat with Pete about the use of sleeping pills here in the home. I want to know how they are stored, who has access to them, and whether any have gone missing recently."

Horace patted Marjorie's hand. "I see what you're thinking. If you, I, and Victor were all drugged, it stands to reason that someone is using stock from the home. Consider it done."

Marjorie smiled gratefully at her friends, appreciating their willingness to follow her lead.

Once they had finished lunch, they separated, each focused on their tasks. Marjorie's eyes drifted towards Ruby's office. All was quiet.

Apollo stopped preening himself and looked her way. "GET TO JACKIE'S! GET TO JACKIE'S."

Marjorie couldn't believe her ears! That bird was psychic. If she wasn't careful, he would give her away. She hurried outside and made her way back to Jackie's apartment, hoping to have a conversation with Poppy and the deceased's niece. As she approached, she was pleased to find the door slightly ajar. They must have arrived.

Marjorie pushed it open, calling out softly as she entered. "Hello?"

There was no response, but she heard movement coming from the rear sitting room where she had been with Isabelle and Horace earlier. As she entered, her stomach dropped at discovering Diana rummaging through the sideboard where Jackie had kept her correspondence and cheque books.

"Diana!" Marjorie exclaimed. "What are you doing here?"

Diana whirled around. "Oh, hello, Marjorie, I was just, erm, tidying up a bit. Trying to help." She closed the drawer hurriedly, hiding something behind her back.

Marjorie's eyes narrowed. Something didn't feel right about Diana's presence, or her nervous behaviour.

"I had hoped it wouldn't be you."

Diana recovered quickly, her face stern. "I don't know what you're talking about, and what do you think you're doing here? You have no right to enter this or any other apartment."

"I was told Poppy Peterbald and Jackie's niece would be here and was hoping to have a chat with Poppy about Miss Bagshaw."

"What do you want to know? Perhaps I can help." Diana

was still making a play at looking like a relaxed and kind care assistant, but the steely glare in her eyes suggested otherwise.

"I wanted to ask her about the inheritance she is soon to receive and whether it came with any conditions."

Diana's reaction was instant, her demeanour turning aggressive. Marjorie had hit the right spot, but she realised she had also put herself in danger. Apollo had tried to warn her. He must have heard Diana saying where she was going.

"And what's the will or its conditions got to do with you?"

"Nothing, but it would mean a lot to my friend Edna to find out why Jackie was murdered."

Diana took a few steps towards Marjorie. "Your *friend* Edna. You've only just met the woman."

The light seemed to dawn on Diana as Marjorie fixed her gaze. "Yes, that's right. Edna is actually my cousin-in-law, as well as a close friend."

"None of this makes any sense, and for your information, Jackie wasn't murdered! I don't know what you think you're doing, or what you think you know, but you need to stop sticking your nose where it doesn't belong." Diana's voice was low and threatening.

Marjorie's heart pounded, but she stood her ground. "I seem to have hit a nerve. Perhaps you could tell me what that is you're holding behind your back?"

Diana's eyes flashed with anger. "It's personal."

"Perhaps I should mention that I was here earlier with Isabelle and Horace and I found the crossed-out cheque. Jackie wanted to help you, didn't she?"

"I've worked hard to get where I am. Of course she wanted to help me; a lot of the residents do." Diana's eyes were ablaze. "It's what I deserve."

"But the rules dictate you can't accept that sort of money from a resident in your care."

"Any money, actually."

Diana had taken a few more steps towards Marjorie, pushing the cheque book she had been holding into a pocket. She was now blocking the exit. Marjorie needed to keep her talking.

"So, when Miss Bagshaw told you she was going to leave half of her estate to the Cat Lady, Poppy Peterbald, you suggested a way around those rules."

"Can't you just accept that she wanted to give me the money? I'm going to be a nurse. You said yourself I'll make an excellent nurse." There was a tremor in Diana's voice.

"We all make mistakes."

"You don't need to be like this. There's no harm done."

"Alas, Diana, there's been plenty of harm done. Jackie Bagshaw was fit and thriving, wasn't she? And you just couldn't wait to get your hands on that money. The money would be a means to getting everything you wanted. Nurse training and your idol's respect."

Diana gritted her teeth, almost spitting the words out. "You're wrong. Jackie had a stroke. The doctor certified it and no-one can prove otherwise. They cremated her earlier today. I was there."

"Why? To make sure she was truly gone? Either way, you and I both know you killed that poor woman."

"Can't you see she was old? She told me plenty of times she'd lived a long life. Mine's just beginning."

"If this is how you view the elderly, you'll never make an excellent nurse, as you put it. If I can't get you for murder, I'll do everything in my power to stop you from getting your hands on any of Jackie Bagshaw's money."

Diana grabbed Marjorie's upper arms, pushing her against a wall until she winced in pain, but did not cry out. "Jackie wanted me to have that money and I'm going to have it. You're not going to stand in my way."

"I would be careful, Diana. Assaulting a resident won't look good on your record, either. It was you who spiked my tea, wasn't it? Why?"

Diana squeezed harder, her face inches from Marjorie's. "Because you didn't obey the rules. People must do as they are told."

Marjorie's mouth opened and closed. "Good heavens! You're deranged. And why did you drug Horace?"

"He was getting in my way. If it wasn't for him, Victor would have died like he was supposed to. Never mind. No-one will believe a confused old lady. I suggest you forget about this for your own good."

Marjorie stared back defiantly. She wouldn't be intimidated.

"Or what? You don't think you can get away with killing three people in the space of a week, do you? Victor died today. I don't suppose you've heard yet, but he did. I couldn't possibly allow someone like you to become a nurse. Who knows what you might do in a position of authority? You've crossed a line, my dear girl, and you should stop now."

Diana's eyes hardened and Marjorie knew she was staring into the depths of the abyss when the carer's hands moved to her throat.

THIRTY-ONE

Horace knocked on Ruby's office door, but Edna didn't wait for a reply. She walked straight in and Horace followed. Pete was sitting there, shoulders slumped as though his world was falling apart.

Edna looked at him. "We need to speak to you."

"Can't it wait?" Ruby snapped.

"I'm afraid not," said Horace.

"Is it about last night? I haven't had the chance to thank you for what you did." Pete's voice was flat as he eyed Horace.

Edna was sick and tired of being left out. "Now look here. None of this would have been uncovered if it weren't for me, so it's time you showed me some respect."

Both heads swivelled towards Edna. Ruby's eyes were narrow, but Pete's were tired, defeated.

"Edna's right," said Horace. "Do you mind if we take a seat?"

Ruby jerked a head towards two chairs. "You might as well, since you're clearly not going to leave."

Edna took another look at Pete and softened. She began by

explaining how she became suspicious when two of her friends died suddenly. Horace and Pete had to intercept many would-be interruptions from Ruby while Edna told her story. Even Ruby stopped frowning when she had to acknowledge that Edna's suspicions about something being amiss had been proved partially right.

"We realise Carl's death was from natural causes, but we're not so sure about Jackie's," Horace added. It was the first Edna had heard about that, but she'd find out later what he meant.

When Fred tapped on the door and joined them, there was a slight pause in the conversation. Ruby huffed impatiently.

"Are we expecting anybody else?"

Fred launched straight in. "Poppy's in the clear. Three people were at work with her that morning, and the night before Jackie died, she was fifteen miles away from here, collecting eight kittens that had been found in a box next to a dustbin. The woman's a saint, from what the man I spoke to told me."

"What about the holiday?" Horace asked.

"Booked months ago, on the threat of divorce from her husband if they didn't get a break. There's no way she could have known what was going to happen back then. She was only told about the contents of the will a couple of days ago and it surprised her as much as anybody."

Pete and Ruby exchanged confused stares. Then Ruby turned to Edna, triumphant.

"You thought Poppy Peterbald had something to do with Jackie's death? That's ridiculous—"

"I'm sorry, I assumed it when I heard about the will," admitted Edna, glumly. "Marge doesn't agree."

"—because she died of a stroke," Ruby muttered. "And who's Marge?"

Ignoring Ruby, Horace turned to Pete. "Which brings us on

to the reason we're here. You're going to find this difficult to accept, but both Marjorie – Edna calls her Marge – and I believe we've had drinks spiked with sleeping pills whilst staying here. It's likely the same person who drugged us did the same to Victor, but with more criminal motives and disastrous consequences. I assume you know he's dead?"

Pete's jaw dropped. "Yes, but wasn't that Hannah? The police have discovered he was taking money from Hannah."

"Hannah's a fool, but she's not a killer," said Horace. "She was a thief trying to pay off her husband's gambling debts with a nasty piece of work threatening to do him harm."

"In which case, she was in an impossible situation," said Frederick. "And I feel sorry for her."

"You would," snapped Edna, but then relented. "Although you've got a point. She can't help having a stupid husband."

Pete rubbed a hand through what little hair he had. "Let me get this straight. You believe someone on my staff is responsible for Victor's death and possibly Jackie's?"

"Yes. So, can you tell us if you've had any drugs go missing?" Edna pressed.

Pete glanced at a glaring Ruby before answering. "Since Shelly's arrest – she's one of our night nurses, the one Horace filmed last night. Anyway, since then, I've done a complete stock check. Shelly ordered medicines and kept the records. In answer to your question, we're missing painkillers, heart meds and sleeping tablets. I was going to let the police know."

"No need," said Edna, spying DS Frame heading their way.

"Ah, just in time, Sergeant," said Horace, smiling.

"I've come from the mortuary. You were right, someone gave Jackie Bagshaw an overdose not of sleeping pills, but of digitalis, which caused her heart to go into a fatal rhythm. The GP had been treating her for atrial fibrillation and assumed she'd had a stroke."

"Which explains why she didn't request a post-mortem?" suggested Horace.

"Well, Pete here has just told us the night nurse was responsible for ordering and monitoring drugs and that some have been going missing," added Edna.

"The nurse has confessed to fixing the medicines logs as well as the stock books, believing Hannah was selling drugs and stock, but Hannah swears she never touched the medication."

"Do you believe her?" Frederick asked.

"Yes, I do. Marjorie asked us to look into the contents of the will and we think we know who the perpetrator is. I need to speak to—"

Before the sergeant got a name out, there was another tap at the door, and Edna recognised Mavis and Poppy from the funeral. They couldn't even open their mouths before Edna jumped up.

"If they're here, where's Marge?"

"What do you mean?" DS Frame asked.

"She went to Jackie's apartment to talk to Poppy."

"I saw Diana going that way a while ago. Perhaps she's chatting to her," said Ruby.

"NURSE AT LAST! NURSE DIANA IN THE MONEY!" Apollo squawked.

Both Poppy and Mavis appeared shell-shocked, but Edna wasn't stopping.

"Hurry!"

Horace, DS Frame and even Fred were all much quicker than Edna, who was left panting like a steam train, but a mixture of adrenaline and concern for her friend gave her superhuman strength. She overtook Fred at the door and was inside Jackie's apartment just in time to witness DS Frame and Horace containing a feral Diana Ferrett and subduing her enough to allow her to be handcuffed.

Edna and Fred grabbed Marjorie's arms before she could fall to the floor, helping her to an easy chair.

"It's okay, Marge, we're here."

"So I see," Marge gasped. The twinkle in her bright blue eyes told Edna she was going to be okay.

THIRTY-TWO

After the excitement of the day, Marjorie was ready to go home, but as Edna's house wasn't big enough for all four of them to stay comfortably, they were all staying another night at Evergreen Acres, this time for free. Horace's friend, Craig Tavistock, had returned from the Middle East and had come in to thank them all personally for what they had done. He assured Marjorie and Horace he would refund their fees in full.

Marjorie had managed to catch a few words with DS Frame and hear how she persuaded her DI to take Marjorie and Horace seriously by sharing information about their previous exploits. Not wanting to be made to look a fool if he didn't act on their suspicions, he had spoken to Jackie Bagshaw's family and explained the situation, requesting permission for a post-mortem. They had been surprised, but played along by allowing the funeral to go ahead, rebooking the actual cremation for a later date. Marjorie was delighted with the outcome and that the DI had charged Diana Ferrett with two murders and attempted murder, plus theft and conspiracy to defraud a vulnerable resident.

Following the best night's sleep, Marjorie's bags were

packed, and when she arrived downstairs Ruby greeted her with an almost-smile, thrusting an envelope into her hand. Marjorie opened the letter and grinned. Her tests revealed no signs of osteoporosis and the blood results required no further action. She met the others in the small dining room for one more breakfast with Isabelle. Edna's friend Eleanor joined them, too.

"I'm sorry I didn't believe you," said Isabelle.

"In your position, I wouldn't have believed us either," said Marjorie. "You were right to be sceptical."

"So the lovely Diana killed Jackie for money, and Victor because he'd found something in her apartment?"

Marjorie had been mulling this over since waking. "Yes. She'd not been allowed to accept a financial gift for her training from Jackie. Pete told us last night that she'd asked him if she could, and he'd said it was against the rules. He told Jackie the same thing. You and I saw the struck-through cheque, and assumed that's what had happened. What we didn't realise was that on hearing that Jackie was going to leave a vast amount of money to Poppy because of her love for cats, Diana then manipulated her into adding a note for Poppy to pass on the sum of one hundred thousand to Diana, not only to cover her nurse training but to set her up for life. Poppy didn't know about any of this until the solicitor called her to tell her she was a beneficiary."

"But you knew, Eleanor, didn't you?" said Edna.

"Yes, Jackie told me that she was leaving a large sum to Poppy for the cat rescue."

"But you weren't aware of the money earmarked for Diana?" Marjorie quizzed.

"No. Not that part."

"That grand scheme was to be kept secret. There was a clause in the letter to Poppy for that fact," Marjorie said. "I'm not sure whether Victor found anything significant in Jackie's apartment. Although I suspect he saw the same cheque Isabelle and I saw and wrote about it in his notebook. We'll never know whether he found anything else because Diana destroyed those pages. Victor was fumbling around trying to be the detective he had once been and his eyes were firmly fixed on Darren, who he believed to be a murderer who had already got off once. DS Frame assured me Darren had a strong alibi for the night his mother-in-law died and that he had been close to her. His former colleagues told the DS Victor wouldn't let it go."

"Stubborn man," said Isabelle, dabbing an eye with a handkerchief.

"It was Darren making a scene about what Victor had been up to that alerted Diana, which set in motion her next attack. She was determined nothing and no-one would stand in the way of her fulfilling her childhood dream. Victor trusted her like everyone did and took the nightcap she made him, most likely under the pretence of offering her support after Darren's outburst."

"But if he'd seen the cheque, he should have been suspicious," said Isabelle.

"I fear he wasn't as sharp as he liked to think he was," explained Marjorie. "He was so obsessed with Darren being his man, he couldn't see beyond it."

"She didn't need to stuff meat down his throat." Edna scowled. "That was cruel."

"No, but she wanted to make it look like suicide or an accident. And let's face it, Diana Ferrett is a scheming murderer who felt she could do anything she wanted."

"Although I miss him dearly, I'm pleased Victor's not here to face charges for extorting money from the beleaguered Hannah McManus."

"I can't help feeling sorry for her," said Frederick.

"So you said," Edna snapped.

"I'm going to miss you four," said Isabelle.

"Me too," added Eleanor.

Edna giggled. "Don't worry. I'll come back and visit."

Cook appeared from the kitchen, placing a couple of bottles of champagne on the table along with six glasses. "Compliments of the manager." She aimed a wink at Marjorie.

"I wasn't expecting a champagne breakfast," said Marjorie.

"Only the best for you lot," said Cook, beaming.

"Yeah, don't knock it, Marge."

After Horace had poured their drinks, they all raised their glasses.

"It appears the awesome foursome has done it again!"

"AWESOME FOURSOME! DONE IT AGAIN. AWESOME FOURSOME!"

Marjorie felt it was right Apollo got the last word. A cackle of laughter rang around the table, along with a few joint snorts from Edna and Horace. It was good to be with friends.

A LETTER FROM THE AUTHOR

Thank you for reading *Murder in a Care Home*. I hope you enjoyed Lady Marjorie and friends' latest outing.

If you want to hear about all my new releases with Storm Publishing, sign up here:

www.stormpublishing.co/dawn-brookes

And if you want to keep in touch about all my books, and receive bonus content, sign up here:

www.dawnbrookespublishing.com/subscribe

If you enjoyed this book and could spare a few moments to leave a review that would be hugely appreciated. Even a short review can make all the difference in encouraging a reader to discover my books for the first time. Thank you so much.

The Lady Marjorie Snellthorpe Mystery series follows a spirited quartet of octogenarians who prove that age is no barrier to sleuthing. Led by Lady Marjorie Snellthorpe, they bring decades of life experience and distinct social backgrounds to the world of crime-solving.

United by their sharp minds and a shared love for justice, they navigate their differences with humour and heart. Though they may not always agree, when it comes to solving murders, they're an unstoppable force.

I created this series to celebrate the wisdom, humour, and

resilience that come with age, showing that even in their golden years, these four are far from done with adventure.

Thanks again for being part of this amazing journey with me and I hope you'll stay in touch – I have so many more stories and ideas to entertain you with.

Dawn Brookes

- facebook.com/dawnbrookespublishing
- tiktok.com/@dawnbrookesauthor
- youtube.com/dawnbrookespublishing
- bookbub.com/authors/dawn-brookes

ACKNOWLEDGEMENTS

Thank you to my scrutiny team for the suggestions and amendments in the early stages.

Thanks to editor Alison Jack for her fine-tuning of this book.

A special thanks to Naomi Knox and the team at Storm Publishing for their support and for helping to bring the books into the hands of new readers.

Thanks for everyone who has supported me in my author journey so far. I couldn't do it without you!

Printed in Dunstable, United Kingdom